Defying the Dragon

Julie Parker

This is a work of fiction. Names, characters, places, and incidents are products of the author's imagination or are used fictitiously and are not to be construed as real. Any resemblance to actual events, locations, organizations, or persons, living or dead, is entirely coincidental.

World Castle Publishing, LLC
Pensacola, Florida
Copyright © Julie Parker 2022
Paperback ISBN: 9781956788525
eBook ISBN: 9781956788532
First Edition World Castle Publishing, LLC, February 14, 2022
http://www.worldcastlepublishing.com
Licensing Notes
Cover: Karen Fuller
Editor: Maxine Bringenberg

For Gary.
The forever hero in my real-life story.

Chapter 1

England, 1347

"I think Aras would be a fine name for our son," Merick said.

Melanie rolled her eyes. Her dour expression thankfully went unnoticed by her companion as they both lay upon their backs looking up at the blue sky. "Perhaps we should be joined in matrimony before we name the children we are to have, my lord."

Merick rolled onto his side and propped himself up on an elbow. "We are betrothed," he reminded her.

"Aye, that we are."

"And I think a fall wedding would be grand."

Melanie closed her eyes and stifled a sigh. She was besieged by guilt, for what sensible maiden would not leap at the chance to wed with such a loving, kind, and thoughtful man as Merick de Balan? It was true he was a second son, but his family was a noble one, and her inevitable in-laws were actually quite likeable. His family could also boast of several fine holdings, one of which Melanie was certain would be bestowed upon her and Merick when they finally wed. She should be resigned to the idea of wedding him by now, but even that word *resigned* plagued her many a sleepless night.

"Rest later, my love. For now, Father and Mother await us to discuss our pending nuptials."

Melanie sat up quickly, having forgotten that her own parents were even now probably arriving at Balan Castle for a weekend of wedding planning. Melanie had arrived earlier with two of her father's men-at-arms as her escort, preferring to ride her own mare and not to sit in the cart with her mother. "Gracious, Merick! I fear I had forgotten for a moment."

Merick was not displeased with her response, for he was certain the love of his life had found his company so agreeable that the reason for this weekend had slipped her mind. Though it was not a rare occasion for their families to come together. Over the years, they had spent many weekends at each other's estates, for they bordered alongside the other. The young couple had practically grown up side-by-side and had been betrothed in childhood by their eager parents. Melanie was Gordon and Fiona Worth's only child, whereas Merick had an older brother who had also been betrothed at an early age to a neighboring estate's young heiress.

Merick rose to his feet and brushed the grass from his breeches. He reached down to offer Melanie his hand when he saw her attempting to stand. As he raised her up, he pulled her closely to his chest and dipped his head low to seek her sweet rosy lips for a kiss. Melanie demurely turned her head, and Merick's lips fell upon her cheek instead.

"Please, Merick, someone may be watching."

It was now Merick's turn to roll his eyes, for always had

Melanie played the chaste and virtuous maiden with him. It was a rare occasion indeed when he was allowed to take any liberties with her no matter how small, despite their betrothal. In the past, he could explain away her hesitance by her youth and inexperience, but lately, Merick felt what could only be described as indifference from Melanie. He could not fail to notice how distant she became whenever he mentioned their upcoming marriage or the children he wished them to have.

Melanie started to descend the rolling green hill they'd rested upon, and Merick took a few quick strides to catch up beside her. He felt slightly appeased when she tucked her dainty hand in the crook of his arm.

"Might we go around the village, Merick?" Melanie asked him softly, with a touch of trepidation in her voice. Her steps slowed as they reached the bottom of the hill and began walking toward the roadway. From there, they could see the outskirts of the small village ahead, and no doubt Melanie did not wish to witness a repeat of that morning's unfortunate events.

The village wasn't a large one. However, it could boast of the finest alehouse for miles around. Young men from neighboring estates took great delight in overindulging themselves, much to the dismay of the poor villagers and anyone else the drunkards lay their sights upon. This morning, although it had only been scant hours past the break of dawn, a group of rowdy youths had already gathered in and around the alehouse. It had been unfortunate that just as Melanie and Merick had been trying to pass by unnoticed, a tussle had broken out, and one of the young men had been thrown right into Merick. Merick, slim and lacking in strength, had fallen to his knees from the blow. Taking great offense, he had risen to his impressive height of six foot three and towered over the miscreant. It had not taken long, however, for the other fellow to notice the lack of confidence behind Merick's threatening anger, and it had not gone well for him. Merick had been lucky to avoid a sound thrashing but had to bear the brunt of a bruised ego when Melanie stepped forth and begged for his life. What began as a pleasant stroll had turned into an ugly and embarrassing scene. The two had quickly gone on their way amidst a riot of cajoling and lewd suggestions aimed at them both.

Merick had no wish to be humiliated again, and Melanie's gentle suggestion was quickly taken to heart. He led her off the roadway and onto a trail through the forest around the village. It wasn't that he was afraid of facing the alehouse troublemakers, for he was no coward. It was just that it was better not to place his beloved in the way of danger, he assured himself. When Balan Castle came into view, Melanie breathed a sigh of relief. She had been tense and slightly wary as they walked along the overgrown pathway through the forest. The trouble this morning might have been more easily forgotten if it had just been a chance happening, but it had been going on for as long as Melanie could remember.

As children, when they'd had the misfortune of running into boys roaming together from other nearby holdings, Merick had always seemed to be the unfortunate butt of their many pranks and jokes. Plagued endlessly and mercilessly, it had almost always fallen to Merick's older brother Desmond and even to Melanie to put an end to the teasing. Melanie had tussled and scraped her way through many a weekend in the company of her betrothed, giving the bullies an impressive show of her strength and skills. But over the years, the boys had grown bigger and stronger, while Melanie, after her thirteenth year, had stopped growing except for gaining inevitable womanly curves. It had become harder and harder to wrestle the boys away from Merick, and she had grown more and more reliant upon Desmond's help.

As they approached the thick wooden doors of the castle, they were suddenly thrown wide as Desmond stepped outside. The sight of him, so big and broad, had always made Melanie feel irresistibly drawn to him, despite the fact he would soon be her brother-in-law.

Seeing his younger brother and Melanie brought a feeling of relief to Desmond, as he had only just heard of the trouble they had encountered in the village that morning. A servant had seen the incident and had quickly relayed the story to Lady de Balan's maid, who in turn eventually relayed the tale to her mistress. Lady de Balan had gone straight to Desmond and appealed to him to seek out his younger brother and Melanie and bring them home safely.

"Merick, I was just coming to find you," Desmond said to the pair. "Melanie." He dipped his head in greeting to his soon-to-be sister-in-law.

Melanie blushed prettily as she smiled at him in response. Where she was glad for Desmond's presence, Merick was not.

"What do you want, Desmond? Didn't Mother tell you Melanie and I would be enjoying a stroll this morning?" Merick snapped at his brother.

Desmond ignored Merick's tone, for he well knew how his brother hated it when he had to be rescued. Fortunately for Desmond, the truth supplied him with a convenient excuse. "I only wanted to tell you that Melanie's parents have just arrived and are now settling into their rooms." His easy smile hid any deception Merick might have suspected.

~*~

Mollified by Desmond's explanation, Merick gruffly thanked his brother and led Melanie inside. Melanie hurried off to greet her parents while Merick climbed the stairs to the solar to seek out his mother. As he expected, Alaine was seated before the large window bent over her needlepoint. She raised her head as she heard Merick's approach.

"Mother," he greeted her, bending to kiss her cheek.

"Hello, darling. Did you meet up with Desmond?" Alaine asked casually.

Merick sat down awkwardly beside her, his large size out of place on the dainty chair. "Do you mean did Desmond once again snatch me from the jaws of danger?"

"Oh, don't be so melodramatic, dear. You know your brother cares only for your welfare."

"Aye, though I wish he would stop being so overly concerned and let me take care of my own problems. My word, Mother, I can handle myself quite well, you know."

Alaine lifted her gaze from her work and looked pointedly into her son's eyes. "The way I heard it told, Melanie had to beg for your life."

Merick rose angrily to his feet. "If I'd had my bow, it would have been a different story!"

"I'm sure you are the finest archer in the land, my dear," Alaine assured him.

"Though I had not thought I'd need to bring a bow and quiver of arrows along when I took my betrothed for a simple stroll," Merick said spitefully.

"Unfortunately, my son, there is no such thing as a simple stroll any longer. Not since that cursed alehouse was erected in the village."

Merick began to pace. "I vow, Mother, if it's the last thing I do, I'll see that wretched place burned to the ground and all the vagabonds it caters to run out of town."

"Ah, that would be a pleasant sight." Alaine sighed.

Before Merick could continue with his plans for revenge, a knock sounded on the open door. "Excuse me, my lady," the young servant said. "Lord de Balan asks if you would please join him and your guests in the hall for the midday meal."

"Gracious, is it that time already? Come, Merick. Let us enjoy a meal before going over the details of your nuptials."

Merick offered his mother his arm and escorted her to the hall, where their guests had just taken their seats at the raised table. He seated himself between Melanie and her mother, Lady Fiona.

"Greetings, my lady, my lord," he said, inclining his head toward his future in-laws.

"Greetings, my boy," said Lord Gordon Worth, as his wife smiled sweetly at Merick.

Merick lifted his cup to his lips as he basked in the warm glow of his loving in-laws. To them, he was no awkward young man who needed endless rescuing. In their eyes, he was perfection. His manners and charm rivaled the awe of the fiercest of knights. He had nothing to prove when he was in their presence. His great love and affection for their only daughter impressed them far more than any brave deeds he would ever display on the field of battle.

Merick's peaceful moment was interrupted by the late arrival of Desmond. His brother strutted forth through the great hall amidst the boisterous calls of his fellow knights and the sighs of young ladies. Desmond took his seat between his father and Lord Worth and reached directly for the ale with one hand and a hunk of bread with his other. "Greetings." His voice was muffled, his mouth overflowing with a large bite of food.

"Desmond, dear, must you shove food into your mouth

so?" Alaine gently chastised her oldest son. "Can't you be more mannerly, like your brother?"

"Mother, please," both boys groaned.

After the meal was finished, the families gathered in the de Balan's spacious drawing room to make wedding plans. Each set of parents was determined the date would be set in the early fall. It just being the middle of spring right now would allow more than enough time for preparations.

"We could make the announcement after the tournament," Lord Worth suggested. Neighboring estates took turns holding the July tournament, this year the task falling to the de Balan's.

"Yes. What a fine idea, my lord," Alaine agreed.

"Merick, son," Victor de Balan said, noting his son's tense expression. "This year, we shall make the archery contest a grand competition, just like the favored joust. And I've no doubt in my mind as to who shall be the victor."

Melanie clapped her hands together in glee. "Oh, Merick! Your father is right. You are the best archer in all of England. I know you are." Her eyes shined in sudden adoration toward her betrothed. Finally, she thought, Merick would have the chance to prove to everyone, especially those bullies, that he was a worthy opponent. Perhaps then the teasing might finally end, and they could live their lives in peace.

Merick worried slightly there could still be a chance he might not win the contest, for there were no guarantees. But then he looked at his love, his sweet Melanie. The eyes she'd turned on him were so full of admiration that all doubt fled his mind. At last, his betrothed regarded him with something other than pity or embarrassment. Merick became thoughtful for a moment, imagining the moment of glory that he, himself, might finally attain—just like Desmond, who had always been the shining star of the annual games. He and Melanie would stand together above the crowd in the high wooden daises, and his father would make the announcement of their wedding date. Merick would take Melanie's hand in his and wave to the loudly cheering crowd.

After everyone had agreed the wedding would be announced at the tournament, the parents got down to the business of agreeing upon the wedding gifts each would bestow upon the pair. As expected, Merick's parents would give them one of their several holdings. The small but elegant Castle Hadley, just north of Balan Castle, would be home to the new couple. Melanie's parents would fill the stables with six thoroughbred horses and give them a herd of cattle to roam the several acres of fields.

Thrilled with the generosity of both of their parents, Melanie and Merick hugged and kissed them with affection. They asked to be excused and hurried off to stroll together in the gardens to discuss the happy future awaiting them. Melanie was so caught up in the excitement of the moment, she forgot any misgivings she'd had in the past about marrying Merick.

They took a seat amongst the roses, and Merick took her hand in his. He looked into her bright blue eyes and admired the beauty of his betrothed. Her hair hung loose to her hips in long blonde waves. Her dress was a flattering green and cut low, showing off the generous curves of her lovely body. She was still very young and innocent, having not yet seen her eighteenth birthday that would fall in autumn. Merick couldn't wait until they were finally joined in matrimony so he may finally sample her charms.

Where Melanie was fair, Merick was dark. His curling, raven black hair just brushed his shoulders, which were broad despite his thin stature. His eyes were dark brown, and when he smiled, he appeared boyishly handsome despite being twenty-and-one.

"Do you think the competition will be fierce at the archery contest?" Merick asked, the slight hitch in his voice betraying his nervousness.

Melanie couldn't help but feel annoyed about Merick's fear. His father had done him a great service by glorifying a game in which Merick excelled, but instead of feeling gratitude, Merick was again wrapped up in his insecurities. "I'm sure you will be fine," she said dryly.

Merick couldn't help but notice the flash of irritation cross Melanie's face. He had done it again. Why hadn't he learned by now that his beloved could not tolerate his want of confidence? Merick stood and made an excuse that he needed to check on something at the stables before quickly leaving Melanie alone in the garden. He could not stand being near her when he knew how distasteful his presence had become to her.

Melanie sighed as she watched him go. The excitement of the last hour suddenly disappeared, and she once again confronted the reality of having Merick for her lord husband for the rest of her life.

Chapter 2

The days and weeks flew by quickly as spring gave way to the hot, dry months of summer. At the week's end, the much-anticipated tournament would begin and continue for two exciting days. Merick had spent every day practicing with his bow and felt confident his skill was unmatched.

Melanie had made preparations of her own, readying herself for her upcoming wedding and life at Hadley Castle. She had almost made peace with the thought of becoming Lady de Balan. Seeing her betrothed only three times since the late spring weekend she'd spent at Balan Castle had helped to make her fate easier to bear. Each time they'd met, Merick had been in the archery field and had a determined air about him. He'd spared her only a perfunctory greeting, almost ignoring her presence, so deep was his concentration. Melanie had found his treatment of her perversely attractive. He usually smothered her with attention during their visits, and she'd secretly likened him to a needy child.

As the weekend of the tournament finally arrived, Melanie

could hardly contain her excitement as she and her parents arrived at Balan Castle. They would be staying in the castle as guests, as would a few others. Spectators and competitors alike were already beginning to set up their tents in the softly rolling fields that surrounded the area. Men practiced swordplay while merchants, preparing to use the event to peddle their wares, erected booths.

Melanie had watched the activities going on through her window high above the castle grounds. She had then dressed for supper and awaited her parents before joining the others in the great hall below. The meal was grand, with over eight courses being served, and didn't end until late in the evening. Afterward, Melanie turned down Merick's offer of a stroll in the garden, opting instead to retire early so she may be well rested for the tournament set to begin tomorrow morning. As she lay in her bed, she found that although she was tired, she was also restless. In two short days, Merick's father would announce their wedding date to all. It wasn't like it would be a great surprise, for everyone in the land knew she and Merick had been betrothed as children. She sighed and rolled over.

Desmond's betrothed had arrived today. His wedding had been announced at the beginning of summer. It was set to take place a month before hers and Merick's. Beatrice Madeon, Desmond's bride to be, had arrived in all her splendor. Though spending only the weekend at Balan Castle, she'd had her servants pack a cart high with her trunks and bags. Beatrice, being one year older than Melanie, had been matched with the de Balan's older son, whereas Melanie had been betrothed to the younger. The soon to be sisters-in-law were polite to each other but had never been close. Beatrice seemed to take cruel delight in extolling the virtues of her betrothed while laughing over the ineptness of Merick. She was, however, always clever enough to only show her sharp tongue whenever she and Melanie were alone. When others were in the room, Beatrice became the epitome of sweetness, and Desmond and his parents were of the assumption she could do no wrong.

Melanie rose early the morning of the tournament and dressed in haste. She knew the games would not begin until the de Balans had taken to the stands, as they were the hosts, but she wanted to be well on her way before Beatrice awoke. She crept out of her room and padded past Beatrice's door before hurrying to the stairway. Once below, she headed straight for the kitchens, hoping Cook would be awake and busy preparing breakfast. She was greeted by the sweet smell of baked bread and fresh summer fruit, piled high on trays upon the wooden table, ready to be served to the guests when they awoke. Cook smiled at Melanie indulgently when she saw her reach for the soft, fresh bread.

"You're up early this morning, my lady."

Melanie didn't sit down on the stool before her to eat, being in too much of a hurry this morning for idle chatter. "Aye. Have you seen any others about yet?"

"Nay, only yourself."

Melanie was about to say it would be a long while yet before *Princess* Beatrice made an appearance, but bit her tongue. She picked up an apple and bid Cook farewell as she left the room. Outside, the day that greeted her was cloudless and warm. Melanie was glad she'd opted to wear only a light cloak over her dress. She could always shed it later at her seat in the stands as the day grew warmer.

Where the castle was silent, the yard was bustling with activity. Lads were readying horses, which had been boarded in the de Balan stables, while young men sat sharpening swords.

Melanie wound her way around visiting knights noisily boasting of their skills before passing beneath the portcullis. There was a huge field set aside for the tournament. High stands had been erected to witness the joust and gave view to the archery field.

Between the castle and the tournament grounds, several colorful tents had been erected. Melanie walked by, noticing the inhabitants were already busy preparing for the day's events. Knights visiting from other castles sat silently as their servants saw to their care and comfort. A giant of a man sat shirtless, wearing only his breeches while his squire carefully shaved his face. He winked at Melanie as she passed by him, and she flushed bright red and turned her eyes down quickly.

"Melanie!" She heard her name being called. She turned toward the sound and saw Merick rushing up to greet her. He held her at arm's length while Melanie smiled up at him.

"Why are you up and about so early?" he asked her, concern etched in his features.

"I'm just anxious for the tournament to begin, my lord." She had no wish to tell Merick she was avoiding Beatrice.

"I had trouble sleeping in as well," Merick admitted. He tucked her hand beneath his arm and began leading her away, not liking the way the shirtless knight was staring at them. "Have your parents risen yet?"

"Nay, I do not believe so." She wasn't certain, for she'd been in such a rush to leave the castle that morn.

Merick wanted some privacy with Melanie, as they'd yet to spend any time alone together since her arrival. He steered her away from the field and walked toward the forest trail. The path was silent except for the sounds of small creatures scurrying around the forest floor or rustling in the treetops. They walked on, enjoying the peaceful surroundings, knowing the area would soon be filled with sounds of swords clashing and people cheering. Merick led them to a clearing, which overlooked a small pond. The sun danced upon the surface of the water, making it sparkle like diamonds.

"Oh, how pretty," Melanie exclaimed.

Merick smiled as he led her over to sit on a smooth rock face that jutted out toward the water like a wide bench. "Careful not to wet your dress," he said.

Melanie tucked the fabric under her legs, her feet dangling toward the small pool, as Merick slid over to sit closely beside her. The rock did not allow for much space, and Melanie could not shift over to give him more room. She felt suddenly uncomfortable at their proximity and wondered what Merick might be up to bringing her here to this place. Merick reached for her hand as they sat quietly together.

Melanie looked at the water and the surrounding forest, the birds in the trees, anywhere but at her betrothed. Since her arrival, she had only seen Merick in the great hall to take their meals or in passing at the castle. She was disappointed that he had failed to stir in her the same excitement he had created when she'd seen him practicing for the games. Then he had been all sweaty and aloof, barely sparing her a glance. What was wrong with her that she would care to be with such a man, Melanie wondered? Perhaps she only craved that which she did not have or that which was hard to get? She had never worried about finding a mate, for it was known to her from the time she could walk that she and Merick would be married. Every woman craved a home and a family with the man she loved, and Melanie had always been assured these things. She did love Merick. She was certain of it. But they had grown up so closely, almost as though they were siblings, and she feared she loved him as a sister loved a brother.

"Shall we sit together in the stands today?" Merick asked.

"Of course," she replied, for it would be expected of her to sit with her betrothed when he was not participating in the games. The archery contests would be played late in the afternoon today, eliminating contenders until the last game on the morrow. Until then, they would watch the others compete from their seats, sheltered safely above the field.

Desmond would be upon the field.

That was the reason Melanie was so quick to elude Beatrice this morning, for she had no wish to listen to her boast of Desmond's merit. Not while Merick sat watching the tournament with the ladies. She would seek Beatrice out when it came time for Merick to show his skill with the bow and arrow.

"Does something amuse you, my dear?"

Melanie blushed slightly for having been caught thinking about the look on Beatrice's face when Merick beat everyone at the archery contest. It was almost always Desmond who won honors each year and came out victorious at the end of the tournament. There was no doubt, Melanie thought, that this year's games would end the same way. Only this time, Merick would also be a champion.

"I'm just thinking about the archery contest," Melanie said innocently.

Merick smiled confidently, he too anxiously awaiting his moment of triumph.

Their shared moment of anticipation of Merick's glory was interrupted by a voice from behind the trees. "Well, if it isn't the lord's son lounging about while others prepare themselves for the tournament."

"Aye, don't you know, Sam, that Merick fears the

battlefield, even if 'tis but a game?" said another voice.

Merick quickly slid from the rock onto the ground beside him. "Who's there?" he demanded, walking toward the sound of the voices.

Elden and Sam Montrose, brothers from a neighboring estate, stepped into the clearing and stood before Merick. They regarded him with sneers and began to walk with calculated steps around him, looking him up and down. Merick was all too aware of the animosity aimed at him. He knew these young men, for they had plagued him endlessly throughout his years.

"Look, Sam, he's not alone," observed Elden, spying Melanie upon the rock. She had struggled ungainly to her feet, hampered by her long dress and the small surface she stood upon.

"I asked you a question," snarled Merick, turning the brothers' attention back to him. Being only two of them, Merick felt certain he could handle them, for the Montrose brothers were both a good head shorter than himself.

But then two others stepped forth from the brush.

Two rough young men from the village came to stand beside the brothers, and the cruel looks upon their faces showed they were of ill intent. Before Merick knew what they were about, they formed a crude circle around him and began to shove him back and forth.

Melanie jumped from the stone and rushed forward, determined to put an end to the torment. She pushed her way around the men and stood in front of Merick.

"Melanie, what are you doing?" demanded Merick.

"You will leave him be! I will not have you manhandling my betrothed!" Melanie hissed, her eyes flashing angrily.

One of the village youths reached out and ran a dirty finger down her cheek. When Melanie slapped his hand away, he tipped back his head and laughed. "Oh, ho! What spirit you possess, my lady," he said admiringly. "And what beauty. What do you see in a spineless boy such as he?" His fellow cohorts howled over the outrage on Merick's face.

"Touch her again, and I shall kill you," Merick threatened.

"What's that, Lord Spineless? Touch her again?" asked Sam. He reached out and grabbed Melanie's wrist in a painful grip, wrenching her away from Merick.

Melanie slammed into Sam's chest. His thick arm wrapped around her waist while his hand still held her wrist captive. When Merick lunged to save her from Sam's vile clutches, the others held him back.

"You will let me loose!" insisted Melanie, fear becoming evident in her voice.

"Not before I taste your sweet, sweet lips, my lady," Sam purred.

Showing a burst of strength, Merick wrenched himself from his attackers and pulled Melanie free of Sam's grip. He pushed her lightly aside. "Run, Melanie!" he told her. He swung his fist, but before it could connect with Sam's jaw, the others were on him again. The village youths latched onto his arms, and Sam and Elden began taking turns punching Merick's face and stomach.

"Stop it! You're killing him!" screamed Melanie, rushing forward to strike the brothers with her own small fists.

Elden grabbed Melanie by her shoulders, his fingers biting into her flesh, and forced her to look at Merick. "Look at him. He is nothing. He cannot even protect you!"

Melanie gasped when she saw Merick, bent from the blows to his stomach, his face swollen and bloodied. Worst of all was the look of defeat on his face. She felt truly frightened in that instant, for she knew all hope was lost. He had given up and resigned them both to their fate.

"Let us go," Melanie begged, trying to gain compassion from Elden.

"I think not, my lady. Too long have we awaited this moment," Elden said.

"Aye," agreed Sam. "For always, Desmond rushes forward to save his precious brother, but not today. Today he is too busy preparing for the tournament. Nay, the Great Knight, will not be riding in to save the day."

"I think the lady asked you to let her go," came a deep voice from behind them.

Melanie turned her head to see who had appeared, as did the others whose curiosity was aroused. There, standing in the clearing, stood the huge knight Melanie had seen outside his tent. The one who had worn no shirt. He was now fully dressed in a tight leather jerkin and leggings. His thick arms were crossed, and his legs were braced far apart as though he prepared to do battle. So still and calm he stood, as though he had not just intruded onto a scene of mayhem. It appeared not to bother him he was outnumbered four to one. His black eyes stared challengingly at the men before him.

"Run along," sneered one of the youths from the village, dismissing the intrusion.

The knight cocked his head and looked at the youth curiously. "Pardon? I seem not to have heard you correctly."

"Ye heard me jus' fine!" the villager retorted. He released his grip on Merick's arm and stepped forward, causing Merick to fall to his side.

Melanie tried to go to him, but Elden still held her tightly.

"He said *run along*," said the other youth from the village.

He, too, released Merick and came up to stand alongside his friend.

Sam took up a stance beside the other two, leaving only Elden, who refused to let go of Melanie.

"Since there are only four of you, I'm willing to show mercy and let you leave. As long as you do it *now*," the knight stated.

He had stressed the word "now" with deadly intent, and Melanie felt a shiver run down her spine. Who was this man, she wondered? And why would he be willing to risk his life for her and Merick? She had never seen him before today, but there he stood, ready to defend them as though he were their champion. And indeed, he did appear a champion. She had thought Merick to be overly tall and Desmond to be large and formidable, but not compared to this warrior.

The men around her either missed the fire in the knight's eyes or foolishly ignored it, thinking their number exceeded his might.

But they were wrong.

Before Melanie had a chance to blink, the knight pulled forth a dirk from his boot and aimed it straight and true, right into Elden's arm that held her. Elden released his grip and howled in pain. Next, the knight's booted heel kicked out and connected with the side of Sam's head, bringing him crashing to the ground. The village youth ran forward to rush him, but the knight lowered and spun around, sweeping his feet out from under him before coming down hard on his chest with an elbow. The last of the four took one look at his wounded friends scattered amongst the dirt and backed away before turning and rushing off into the trees.

Melanie could hear the sound of his terrified steps on the

forest floor, running desperately for his life. She looked into the knight's eyes and whispered, "Thank you," before hurrying to Merick's slumped form. She lifted his bruised head onto her lap and brushed his hair tenderly from his brow.

"I don't know how we can ever thank you for saving us," Melanie said to the knight. She again felt a shiver pass through her as he speared her with his dark look.

"I'm sure I will think of a way," he told her quietly before turning to disappear behind the thick wall of trees.

Chapter 3

Merick sat in the stands beside Melanie, overlooking the tournament field. He held a cool cloth to his cheek, hoping to decrease the bruising, which was becoming more pronounced as the day wore on. In one short hour, he was expected to compete on the archery field. He had no choice but to attend if he were to continue on the morrow. He'd been looking forward to demonstrating his skill, up until the time he'd been painfully reminded of what a milksop he was. His pride and his body had taken such a beating, he was now hesitant about putting himself on display, fearful he might again fail.

He still was uncertain of what had transpired earlier after the men had attacked him, for his memory was hazy. He remembered awakening in the clearing by the pond. Melanie had held his head in her lap while a cloth dipped in the cool water from the pond rested on his brow. He looked at the cloth now and realized it was a piece of material ripped from Melanie's chemise. He had no memory of falling to the ground. When he had asked Melanie where the men had gone, she vaguely explained that they'd run off. Merick had been relieved, for he'd seen the looks they had aimed at his beloved, and he remembered being so fearful they might make ill use of her. But she sat glowing beside him, seemingly unharmed and unfazed by the events, practically oblivious to his suffering, so engrossed was she in the games unfolding before them.

Merick looked down at the tournament grounds expecting to see Desmond, for Melanie seemed to take special delight in watching his brother compete. Desmond was upon the field, seated on his horse with a lance poised in his hand preparing for the joust, but it was not he her eyes were drawn to. It was the knight at the other end of the field who had all of Melanie's attention.

The man appeared vaguely familiar to Merick. He was certain he'd seen him before, but he knew not from where. When his name had been announced, the crowd had grown silent and then cheered uproariously. It seemed they had King Edward's own champion on their field, Lord Jamie de Brock, the Dragon. Now returned from France, de Brock had fought alongside the Black Prince in the battle of Crecy a year ago. It was rumored he'd even saved the young prince's life. Apparently, they'd been traveling at night when their small band had been attacked. The prince, caught unawares, had fallen, and de Brock had rushed forward to protect him. It was said he held attackers at bay with his sword and by spewing mouthfuls of wine through the flame of a torch. It had given the impression he was breathing fire from his very lungs, thus giving him the name Dragon. Soon after returning home, he'd been gifted Tenebrous Castle for his bravery.

Merick remembered seeing the castle once on a trip with his father and Desmond. It towered over five stories high, seeming to jut forth from the ground beneath it like a giant steel sword. Surrounded by a tall curtain wall of heavy stone and acres of thick forest, it had appeared impenetrable. Though grand, it had a coldness about it, appearing dark and gloomy, living up to its name, Tenebrous. It had seemed a strange gift to Merick for a knight who'd had the gratitude of a king.

Merick broke from his reverie, his attention suddenly drawn to the field below when he heard the blast of a horn. The flags were dropped, and the horses took flight down the length of the field, the riders leaning forward, preparing to strike in the pass. As they neared each other, the knights braced against the blows, shattering their lances to splinters against the other's breastplates. The noise was sickening to Merick, who shivered as he watched the men rein in their mounts. They turned round and took up another lance handed over by their squires, preparing to ride out again. Merick was relieved it was not he on the field who faced de Brock. He had to admit that even Desmond appeared ill-matched against the man.

Melanie ran her tongue over her lips, which had suddenly gone dry. She held her breath as she watched the riders take another stunning blow from the lances as they thundered past each other. She exhaled slowly when she saw they both were still seated upon their mounts and returning to opposite ends of the field. There, they took up another lance and then sat poised and ready to ride out again. Their horses stomped their hooves in frustration while awaiting the command to charge. Moments later, the flag was dropped for the third time.

This time as the knights rode toward each other, de Brock did something Melanie, in all her life, had never seen before. Instead of using his lance to unhorse his opponent, he dropped the weapon at the last second, bent low, and spun round backward in his saddle, stretching out his right leg. His booted heel caught the unprepared Desmond square in the chest and sent him sprawling to the ground.

The crowd went wild. They rose to their feet, some crying foul, others delighted with the show they had just witnessed. Desmond lay on his back in the dirt but soon sat up and looked around himself, confused over what had transpired. His eyes sought out his opponent, whom he finally spied across the field dismounting his horse. Dragon was handed his sword, and once he clasped it in his firm grip, turned toward Desmond and began stalking forward. Desmond was on his feet by the time de Brock reached him. His squire had seen the intent of the other knight, and he now rushed forward on shaking legs toward his master, keeping a wary eye on de Brock, to hand over Desmond's sword.

The men raised up their sword hilts, giving a brisk salute before engaging in battle. The blades were dull but still appeared deadly as they crashed against one another. Desmond fought like a man possessed, slashing through the air skillfully, consumed with his goal of disarming his opponent quickly, as was his style. Dragon, too, fought skillfully, but where Desmond's fight seemed almost desperate, there was a calculated smile upon the lips of Jamie de Brock.

"He's enjoying this," gasped Melanie, who had taken to her feet when Desmond had fallen. She remembered how easily de Brock had handled the three men at the pond and driven the fourth off into the woods. It didn't take him long to disarm Desmond, who had always walked away the victor in every game he'd entered, but now, this time, stumbled to the ground in defeat. And as Dragon stood triumphantly over his opponent, he raised his gaze to the stands to stare up at the cheering crowd. Melanie felt the sudden thrill of excitement and then a wave of fear as the knight's black eyes, filled with blazing intent, fastened upon her.

~*~

"How are you, Brother?" asked Merick as he pulled a chair up beside Desmond's bedside. Beatrice and Alaine stepped from the room to give the men some privacy.

Desmond appeared to be well, though he'd had to be carried to his bed from the tiltyard, unable to hold his own weight with his injured leg. Becoming twisted in his fall in the sword fight, he had come down hard upon it. The physician had been called to check his leg and assured Desmond that he'd recover well before his wedding, but not in time to finish competing in the tournament.

Desmond struggled to sit up, but stopped when the pain overwhelmed him. He looked at his brother's face and was shocked, for he had not yet seen him today. "What the bloody hell happened to you?"

Merick reached up to lightly touch his swollen face. "Had a bit of a run-in with some fellows at the pond this morning. Worry not, for they soon left after having a bit of sport with me."

Desmond snorted angrily. "A bit, you say!"

Merick tried to smile, but the pain in his jaw stopped him. "You're in a foul mood."

"Do you blame me?" Desmond asked angrily. "Not only does de Brock knock me from my horse, but he makes an even bigger mockery of me by turning me lame."

"You're not lame," Merick reminded him.

"I might as well be. What the hell kind of move was that, anyway? He kicked me off my bloody horse!"

"All I can say, Brother, 'tis glad I am I did not have to compete with him at the archery contest."

"Aye, I wish you had fired an arrow into his foot, but then he'd probably have kicked you in the arse. How did you do, by the way?"

Merick's victory seemed somewhat shallow now that his brother lay wounded. "I will continue on the morrow," he said simply.

Desmond reached out his hand and gave Merick a brotherly slap on the back. "Well done! At least one of the de Balan brothers will play on."

Merick regarded his brother as his expression suddenly turned serious. "What is it, Desmond?" he asked, thinking the pain in his leg was bothering him.

"I am worried, Merick, this I must admit," Desmond said. Sweat had begun to bead upon his brow, and as his hand reached toward a cup of ale at his bedside, Merick saw the tremble in his fingers.

"What is it?"

Desmond lifted the cup to his lips and drank deeply. Merick waited patiently as he wiped the sleeve of his shirt across his mouth. He took the cup from Desmond and returned it to the table, anxious yet fearful to hear what his brother might say.

"Did you watch him today on the field?"

"Who?" Merick asked, but he feared he already knew the answer.

"Dragon," Desmond confirmed, his voice little more than a whisper. "He's not human, Brother."

Merick took to his feet and walked to the foot of Desmond's bed, suddenly fearful his brother had hurt more than his leg in the fall. "He's just a man, Desmond."

Desmond's eyes flashed, and he struggled into a sitting position. "It was fortunate that I only had to face him in the joust, for if I'd faced him in any other game, he would have finished me off earlier."

"No, Desmond, you cannot know that for certain," Merick assured him.

"Aye! I do know it. You may not have watched the wrestling match and sword fighting, but I did. Dragon outmatched every competitor he faced. It was just luck that we did not face off before the joust. He seems a man with a purpose. He already has the king's favor and Castle Tenebrous, so I know not what it is he seeks."

It was true that Merick had failed to watch the other games, for he and Melanie had returned late because of his injury. Melanie had even tried to get him to go lie down in his room for a while, but he had insisted he watch Desmond in the joust. Now, as he listened to his brother, a sick feeling began to form in his stomach.

"I guess I should feel fortunate he had no wish to show his skill on the archery field," Merick said.

"Mayhap, it is the only contest he cannot win."

"And it is too late for him to enter now." Merick shrugged his shoulders to demonstrate his lack of concern. He hoped his easy dismissal of de Brock's unknown intentions would reassure Desmond. "I must go. Melanie is probably awaiting me to escort her around the merchant's booths."

"Watch out for him, Brother," Desmond warned.

Merick quietly closed the door to his brother's chamber and started down the hallway. Try as he might, he could not get his brother's words to leave his mind, not when he recalled the heated stare Dragon had given Melanie after the joust.

~*~

Melanie found Beatrice sitting alone in her room with

a hairbrush clasped tightly in her hand, staring off into space. After entering, she turned to close the door softly behind her. She approached Beatrice, who had not yet become aware of her presence.

"Beatrice," she said quietly so as not to startle the young woman.

Beatrice shook suddenly, letting the brush slip to the floor. She stared at it for a moment, then dropped her head into her hands to weep pitifully.

Melanie went to her at once and put her arms around her to give comfort. It took a few minutes before the weeping turned to loud sniffles, and Beatrice seemed to gain control of her emotions.

She gently pushed Melanie away from her. "Pray, Melanie, I fear I do not know what's come over me," Beatrice said with a forced smile, embarrassed to be caught in a moment of weakness.

"'Tis all right to be fearful," Melanie told her. "But the physician assured us the injury is not permanent. Desmond will soon be back on his feet."

Beatrice rose and began to pace around the room frantically. "I know he will heal. It is not his leg that has me worried."

"What is it then?"

"His confidence has taken a beating, I fear. Never before has he been defeated, and so soundly. By God, the shame of it, Melanie. To be carried from his father's own field."

"It will be all right, Beatrice. This will soon be forgotten by all, including Desmond. He will fight again."

"The damage has already been done. Can't you see, you little fool, that I was to be married to an undefeated champion? And now that man is no longer Desmond de Balan. That man is now Lord Jamie de Brock!" she spat.

Melanie hadn't realized until that moment just how self-centered her future sister-in-law was. She was not concerned about Desmond's injury, only the fact that he had been defeated on the field today. Melanie backed away from Beatrice, suddenly fearful of the twisted anger she saw on the young woman's face and turned to rush from the room.

Chapter 4

The hall was close to overflowing that night at supper with guests in attendance for the tournament. The high table seemed overly quiet without Desmond's presence, him taking his meal with Beatrice in his room. Melanie had secretly worried over her future brother-in-law, considering he had not yet realized the perfidy of his betrothed. She had struggled with the idea of going to Desmond's mother, revealing what she had seen and heard. Yet she feared Alaine would explain Beatrice's condition as one of hysterics brought on by stress and worry. She had to bite her tongue during the meal when someone made a comment about what an attentive wife Beatrice would make.

Merick could tell by Melanie's silence throughout the evening that she had much on her mind. He'd tried to gain her attention a number of times during the meal, but she had practically ignored him and everyone else around her. He feared she secretly pined for the great knight she had seen on the field today. It was true de Brock had been a sight to behold, but his beloved's melancholy since the end of the games had made him worry. Perhaps what had happened today at the pond with those men had finally sunk in. Did she reconsider their wedding, fearful that he could not protect her? Did she instead long for an undefeated warrior who could keep her safe? A warrior such as Dragon?

"Walk with me, Melanie?" Merick asked her as supper came to an end, and others began to disperse from the hall. The meal had gone on for almost two hours, and Merick was exhausted from the day's events. He truly wished to just go off to his room and make ready for bed, knowing the day he faced tomorrow would be just as tiring. But spending time with Melanie right now was more important than resting. He had to talk to her if only to reassure himself that all was well between them.

Melanie smiled up at Merick and assented to his request, putting her hand in his as he led her from the great hall. They went outside into the cool night and strolled leisurely, greeting guests as they passed them. Merick led Melanie along the side of the high wall of the castle and paused to lean against the stone below the room she was staying in.

Melanie could tell he was disturbed about something, and though she hated the thought of adding to his burden, she wanted to tell him about Beatrice. He'd had his own doubts about the woman his brother was to marry, and Melanie was certain that if anyone could make Desmond see the truth, it would be he. "Merick, I have something to tell you, and I fear you may not like what I have to say," she began.

Merick closed his eyes and took a deep breath to prepare for Melanie's revelation. He feared she was about to ask to be released from their betrothal so that she may be with de Brock. He'd seen the look they'd exchanged after the joust. The way de Brock's eyes had sought out Melanie. Too, he was now almost certain that the knight he had seen this morning, the shirtless giant who had been staring at them so intently, was de Brock. Had Melanie had a conversation with him this morning? Had she come upon him while she strolled amongst the tents and been captivated by his presence? Though their betrothal was legally binding, Merick knew he would not make Melanie marry him against her will. It would kill him to do it, but if she asked to be released from the agreement, he would set her free. Both of their parents would agree to it if they were to be of the same accord. They loved them too much to see them unhappy.

"Just go ahead and tell me," Merick snapped, suddenly anxious to get the bad news out into the open.

Melanie was startled by Merick's tone. If already he was this upset about something, she couldn't possibly tell him more distressing news. Desmond's condition, not to mention the pressure of competing in the tournament, must have been wearing on him. "'Tis not important. We can discuss it another time," she told him, deciding to wait for a better moment to break the news about Beatrice.

Merick was furious. If she was going to crush his heart to pieces, did she really think it mattered to him if it were later rather than sooner? Why couldn't she just get it over with?

"Please don't be upset. Really, what I have to tell you is something that can wait," Melanie assured him. She reached up to gently touch his cheek, running light fingers over his bruised skin.

Merick closed his eyes and let his thoughts slip away to a time when things had been certain between them. He remembered when he'd first laid eyes upon her, though he'd only been a lad of three. She'd been wrapped tight, cradled in her mother's arms, and he'd stepped quietly up to the lady's chair to peek at the babe. He'd been mesmerized by her sweet beauty even then, though he remembered Melanie had suddenly woken to find his nose poking in her face. The howl she'd let loose had rung in his ears for days. Then she had been a toddling two-year-old, clumsy and full of mischief. She'd wandered outside to the bailey and been chased by chickens behind the barn, and there she'd hidden, crying until Merick had found her. Each time she came with her parents for a visit, she had grown more and more beautiful. From the very beginning, she had enchanted him, and he could not imagine being denied her presence while she lived out the rest of her life. They had grown up together and were supposed to grow old together.

But now, she stood before him, ready to deny him the future between them. "Tell me, Melanie, I beg you. Do not let this linger between us. I would know the truth," he said.

Melanie began to feel slightly annoyed he couldn't just forget about it. Why must he always think when she had something to say it must be urgent? It was as though he could not go on a moment longer until she spoke her piece and allayed his ever-present fears. Would it always be thus between them?

"Must you be so melodramatic, Merick?"

Merick reeled back from her, his hands going to his head in frustration. "Is it wrong of me to hear from your own lips how you plan to end our betrothal?"

Now it was Melanie's turn to become upset. "What?" She must have mistaken his words, but the look on his face was far too serious.

Merick glared daggers at her. He was about to make the supreme sacrifice of letting her go, and she pretended to know not of what he spoke. "I saw the look you and de Brock gave each other after the joust. What is there between you?"

Melanie hadn't realized Merick had witnessed the exchange. But why would he assume there was something going on between the two of them? She stood stunned over the accusation he hurled at her, not knowing how to respond.

Her silence only condemned her in Merick's eyes, and he became even more enraged. "You're planning on leaving with him after the tournament!" It was not a question but an inevitable fact in his mind.

"Are you mad?" Melanie gasped at him.

"I saw you look at him with fire in your eyes, do not deny it!" Merick reached out to grab her by the shoulders. By God, he determined, he would make her tell him the truth.

"If you saw anything, 'twas only shock you witnessed."

"Yes. Shock over how in love you are with him."

Melanie couldn't believe what she was hearing. One exchanged look with de Brock, and Merick was ready to pack her off to marry the man. "No, I was only shocked that 'twas he," she insisted.

"Who, the famous Dragon?"

"No, the man who had rescued us."

The air hung heavy between them. Melanie felt badly. She had not wanted to tell Merick what had really happened at the pond when those men had attacked them, but he was leaving her no choice.

"What say you, Melanie?" His voice was no more than a whisper now. He feared what she would say, but suddenly everything seemed to make sense. When he'd seen de Brock, he had been familiar to him, but it was more than just the passing glance he'd spared him at the tents this morn. It had been as though he'd seen him in a dream.

But it hadn't been a dream.

It had been just before he'd fallen unconscious. He remembered that now. It was how he and Melanie had escaped their terrible fate—thanks to Dragon. It was de Brock who had saved them, while Merick had lain helpless in the dirt, succumbing to his injuries.

Melanie watched the play of emotions on Merick's face as he recalled what had happened to them that morning. "Merick, please, don't be upset. There was naught you could do," she assured him.

Merick looked at her in shock, terrified over what might have been if not for Dragon's timely rescue. And now it seemed de Brock fancied himself in love with Melanie. The look he'd seen on the man's face today was unmistakable. But who was Merick to stand in the way of their union? He could not protect Melanie the way de Brock could. Nay, he should do her the favor of releasing her from their betrothal and allowing her the freedom to choose whom she may.

"I will not stand in your path if you so desire to have de Brock for your husband instead of me. I release you from our betrothal," he told her, then turned and walked off silently into the night, leaving Melanie alone to contemplate his words.

Chapter 5

Melanie sat with her mother in the stands watching the tournament the next morning. She squinted against the glare of the sun reflecting off the knights' shields below. Removing the light gloves from her hands, she rubbed at her tired eyes. Sleep had eluded her last night. She'd tossed and turned, fretting over Merick's parting words. After he'd left her standing alone last night, she'd found her way up to her room and gone to bed. The thought of going after Merick, demanding he explain himself, hadn't even entered her mind. She'd been far too furious.

How dare he say their betrothal was dissolved and she could run off to marry de Brock? As if with the wave of his hand, Merick thought he could magically end their agreement. His audacity had infuriated her. It had been bad enough he'd accused her of having something going on with de Brock, but then to care so little for her that he would just hand her over to him was ridiculous. She had not yet said anything to her parents, but she was tempted to confide in Lady Alaine. Perhaps she could get through to her stubborn son and make him see how daft he was being.

"Melanie!"

Melanie jumped when she heard her mother's voice. "What is it, Mother?"

"Whatever is the matter with you this morning, child? Three times I have said your name, and yet you act as though you were miles away."

Melanie ducked her head to hide her embarrassment. She didn't want to let on to her mother what had happened to make her so pensive. Though she was hurt by Merick's words, she, too, had her pride. "I'm fine, Mother. It's just I had little rest last night."

Fiona nodded her head in understanding. "Ah, you are nervous about the announcement of your wedding date today," she said knowingly.

Melanie nodded her head in the affirmative and breathed a sigh of relief. She'd let her mother think that was what was bothering her.

Fiona gently patted her hand. "Fret not, darling, all will be well."

"I hope so, Mother."

As the tournament played out over the next hour, Melanie had difficulty concentrating on the excitement below. The crowded stands had suddenly become overly hot, and she felt a desperate need to be alone with her thoughts. She looked at her mother's profile and saw the engrossed look upon her face as she watched the games.

"Mother, I wish to partake of refreshments. The heat is stifling up here. Would you like something?"

"That sounds wonderful, dear," Fiona replied, without taking her eyes from the field.

Melanie wound her way through the other spectators in the stands and down the narrow steps to the ground below. Strolling to where the vendors had set up their booths, she bought one cup of sweetened ice for herself and decided to get her mother's later, after she took a short stroll away from the crowds. She remembered the beautiful stream Merick had taken her to and was almost tempted to return there until the faces of the men who had accosted them flashed in her mind. The allure of the cool forest proved to be too powerful as she passed by, and Melanie decided she would be safe enough if she kept to a trail that ran close to the edge of the field.

As she entered the woods, her thoughts again turned to Merick's cool dismissal of her last night. She had wanted to tell him about Beatrice, but he hadn't given her a chance. Instead, he'd shocked her with his outrageous accusations. How could he think there was anything between her and Jamie de Brock? Besides thanking him at the pond for saving her and Merick, she had not said another word to the man. It was true she had looked at him on the field as he jousted, but all eyes had been riveted on the game. She could not deny he had sought her out in the crowd, his hot stare burning into her, but that hardly proved there was something between them.

Melanie shivered slightly with excitement as she recalled how powerful de Brock was. Not only on the field but when he had dispatched those miscreants at the pond with little effort. The trail turned deeper into the forest, but Melanie walked on, distracted by her recollections of Dragon's prowess.

But then another thought entered her mind. She stopped suddenly when the words her mother had spoken earlier replayed themselves. Fiona had asked Melanie if she was nervous about the announcement that would be made after the tournament. The announcement about her wedding date to Merick.

But there wasn't going to be an announcement.

How could there be when Merick had broken things off with her the night before? He may have already spoken to his father about Melanie's suspected treachery. Lord de Balan would be furious, as would Alaine, believing that Melanie would be so shallow and callous as to cast Merick aside after just a few stolen glances at Jamie de Brock.

Melanie sat down hard upon a log at the side of the trail, no longer able to make her shaking legs move forward. What if Lord de Balan was so furious he publicly humiliated Melanie? What if he ordered her and her family to leave his home and never return? Her parents would never get over the disgrace. She must return immediately and tell her mother everything!

She jumped to her feet and began to hurry back down the pathway. It wasn't too late, she assured herself. There was still time to either make Merick see reason, or if that failed, she would convince her parents it was in their best interest to leave for home. She rushed on so quickly that she almost ran right into Jamie de Brock's huge chest when he stepped suddenly out of the trees before her.

Melanie gasped as he caught her just in time in his powerful grip. "My lord! I...I did not see you there. My apologies."

Dragon's smile was feral. "No damage done."

Melanie pulled away from him and stepped back, not liking the curl of his lips or the fire in his eyes. She looked at him a moment longer, then went to step around him to go on her way. "Pray, excuse me, my lord. I must get back to the stands. My mother awaits me there."

Dragon blocked her path. "I think not."

Melanie gaped at his bluntly spoken words. "I do not

think I understand your meaning." She tried to make her voice sound indignant, but she sounded fearful even to her own ears.

His meaning became all too clear when de Brock once again took Melanie into his grip. Before she knew what he was about, he dipped his head low and pressed his hot mouth against hers. Melanie felt as though she were on fire. She grew faintly aware of the feel of de Brock's large hand resting low on her back and pulling her more closely toward him. His kiss was passionate and consuming, unlike the sweet, gentle kisses Merick gave her. When the contact of their lips finally broke, Melanie found herself gasping for air. Once she regained her wits, she roughly broke free of de Brock's hold and slapped him hard across the face.

"How dare you!" she hissed.

Instead of taking offense, de Brock smiled and rubbed his jaw lightly. But then his expression became predatory. Melanie stepped back, but for every step she took, de Brock took one forward. He stalked her like she was his prey, and Melanie suddenly became fearful. She turned and ran, barreling further into the forest and away from the safety of the castle grounds. She had seen this man upon the field and knew what he was capable of. He toyed with her. And foolishly, she had led him on a merry chase—one he could end at any time—and brought herself deeper into danger.

Dragon soon tired of the game and swiftly overtook Melanie's lagging form. He reached for her arm to halt her wild flight and turned her to him. It impressed him greatly that she did not cower or cry. He could see her slight tremble as she faced him defiantly, not willing to allow him to take her willingly.

Melanie closed her eyes, fearing what would happen to her now, for this scene would surely play out only one way. And then, Merick would never want her. Why, oh why, she asked herself, had she not gone to him and demanded they work things out between them? Why had she let her stubborn, foolish pride override her good sense? She had gone and ruined everything. Her life had been laid out before her in all of its splendid glory, but she had treated it callously, taking her good fortune for granted. Now all was lost.

Melanie felt herself being suddenly turned around. She was surprised when she felt her hands being brought together and the feel of a rope pulled snugly around them.

"What are you doing?" she demanded. Indeed, she was relieved, for she had feared the warrior would just throw her to the ground and have his way with her. But then she became almost paralyzed with terror as she realized he meant to do something far more sinister.

"Fear not, my lady," he soothed, not wishing to have a hysterical female on his hands. "I am returning to Tenebrous, and I have decided you shall accompany me," he told her before shoving a rag into her mouth and tossing her over his shoulder.

Melanie kicked and squirmed as de Brock carried her to the horse he had waiting in the forest. He had seen her when she left the stands and then watched as she entered the forest. He had ridden along and entered the forest further down, then tied his horse and gone on by foot. It had not taken him long to find her. Now he would return home, but he would not be alone.

~*~

Desmond lay in his bed, watching Merick pace back and forth between his two windows. A half-eaten tray from breakfast sat at his bedside, the fare suddenly unappealing after Merick's announcement. "What do you plan to do this eve, after the tournament?"

Merick stopped and turned toward his brother. "I was

hoping you could help me think of something to say to Father."

"Other than the fact you are a dolt?"

"You did not see them, Desmond!" Merick insisted. "If you had, you would know I speak the truth."

"So Melanie gazed at de Brock with longing in her eyes, and he, too, looked hotly at her. It wouldn't be the first time Melanie has looked at another. It does not mean she plots to run away with the man!"

"I know what you say," Merick said quietly. "For I have seen how she regards the knights at tournaments. Indeed, I have seen how she regards even you, Brother."

Desmond looked down at his hands folded tightly against his chest. He had suspected his brother knew that Melanie looked at him with something more than sisterly interest. It had troubled him only slightly, though, for he knew how much she loved Merick.

"You must go to her and say you misspoke. Tell her you are sorry, for though you are hurt, you must know you have accused her falsely."

"I did not set her free from our betrothal because I was angry. I set her free because I love her." Merick saw Desmond's questioning look and tried to explain his words. "She looks at me with a forlorn expression on her face. I know I am not the man she wishes me to be. I only released her after I discovered my weakness almost cost her her innocence, and me, perhaps my very life."

"What say you, Brother?" Desmond demanded.

Merick ran a hand through his hair in agitation. He had not wished to relay this part of the tale to Desmond, for he feared his brother's overprotective nature and well knew he would want retribution. "It was Dragon who came upon us at the pond and dispatched the men who accosted Melanie and me. As I lay beaten and senseless, leaving my lady unprotected, it was he who came upon the scene and dispatched the miscreants. As much as I hate de Brock for stealing Melanie's heart, I, too, will owe him a debt of gratitude for as long as I live."

"So you think to repay the man by giving him your betrothed?"

"He can keep her safe. What can I offer her except a life of fear and uncertainty?"

Desmond looked into his brother's eyes. The defeated look on his face wrenched at his heart. "You can give her your love."

Merick walked toward the bedroom door and opened it. "It is not enough," he said before stepping out of the room.

Chapter 6

Merick was striding across the field toward the stands when Lady Worth approached him.

"Merick, my dear. Tell me, have you seen our Melanie?" she asked him.

"Nay, I was just on my way to seek her out. Is she not watching the games?" In truth, he had not laid eyes upon her since they had spoken last eve.

"She left the stands to seek refreshments for us close to an hour ago. She has not yet returned. I thought perhaps she was with you."

Merick felt a slight wave of unease. "Perhaps she has decided to wander the grounds to check out the merchant's wares?"

Fiona looked uncertain. "I suppose she could have, yet I think it strange she did not ask me to accompany her."

Merick knew that Melanie was probably still angry with him, and he couldn't picture her sitting in the stands while she was in a rage. She preferred to walk around as she worked things out. He knew she had much on her mind, but Fiona would not be aware of this. It was obvious Melanie hadn't confided in her. Otherwise, she would not have referred to her daughter as *our* Melanie.

"I will seek her out if it will ease your mind."

Fiona smiled at him adoringly and patted his arm. "You are a dear."

Merick turned and strode in the direction of the merchant's tables. If Melanie were there, he would find her. However, he feared she might instead be in the arms of de Brock, telling him she was now free to be his. He hesitated only slightly before he turned in the direction of the tents of the visiting knights. He found some comfort in the fact that Lord and Lady Worth would not welcome de Brock lovingly into their fold.

As he approached the tent he now knew to be Dragon's, he was surprised to see the man's squire disassembling the canvas. He strode directly before the lad and cleared his throat to get his attention.

"Aye, my lord?"

"Your master, boy. Where is he?"

The lad hung his head a moment, trying to remember exactly what de Brock had told him. "I am to pack up my lord's things and bring them with all haste back to Tenebrous Castle."

Merick was shocked and momentarily speechless. Could it be possible that Melanie had told de Brock to leave her alone? Had her callous dismissal of his blatant admiration driven the man to forgo the tournament and leave for home? Merick could not believe his good fortune.

"He was in a hurry to leave with his lady." The lad gave Merick a sly wink.

Merick looked back at him with a stunned expression.

Surely the lad was mistaken. He could not be speaking of Melanie.

"His...lady?" Merick despised the squeak his voice had suddenly become.

"Aye, my lord. He said they would be leaving right away. Seemed a shame, though. The tournament was almost at an end. I cannot understand why he would leave now."

The lad turned back to his task, shaking his head and mumbling something about troublesome females. Merick stumbled away. In a daze, he walked to the castle and went directly to Desmond's bedchamber. He entered within unannounced.

Desmond was sitting in a comfortable chair before the window. He turned toward the doorway when he heard Merick's approach. He knew immediately by the scowl on his brother's face that something was very wrong.

"I take it things did not go well with Melanie. Did you quarrel again?"

Merick, who had begun to pace the floor, stopped dead. "I cannot quarrel with that which is no longer here."

Desmond looked at him questioningly. "What do you mean?"

Merick began to pace again, his arms gesturing madly in the air to accent his words. "I mean that Melanie and de Brock have run off together!"

"Surely you are mistaken."

"I heard it from de Brock's own squire just now. He was disassembling the tent and making with all haste back to Tenebrous Castle."

"Did you see them depart?"

"Nay. They had already left." Merick sat down in a chair across from Desmond, suddenly feeling drained of all his strength now that the reality of the situation had sunk in. "She's gone, Brother. She has left me for Dragon, just as I told her to do last night."

"I cannot believe Melanie would just leave with a man she does not even know."

"At the pond the other day, he saved her when I could not. And I have seen how they look at each other. Perhaps it was enough for her."

"Did she tell no one?" Desmond demanded.

"Not even her poor mother, who even now awaits her in the stands. I told Lady Worth I would seek out her daughter because she had not yet returned. What am I to say to her?"

"Lady Worth knew naught of what transpired between you two last night then?"

"She referred to her daughter as *our Melanie*. She would not have done so if she knew."

"I suppose you are right," Desmond agreed. "But this all seems so strange and sudden to me. Why would de Brock leave now when he has so much to gain by staying to the end of the tournament?"

"Don't forget that Father was to announce our wedding date tonight. Melanie would not have wanted to stay to face the humiliation of that moment," Merick reminded him.

"Especially if she feared it would not happen. Perhaps she was ashamed of what her parents would think?"

"You're right. I told Melanie I released her from our betrothal. She might not have been able to bring herself to tell her parents there would be no announcement."

"You have not told Mother or Father yet of your decision?" Desmond asked.

"Nay, I was going to tell them today after I spoke with Melanie."

Desmond looked at Merick's ragged expression. There was no doubt his brother was feeling like he drove Melanie into de Brock's arms whether she had wished it or not.

"If only I'd had the opportunity to talk to Melanie this morning. I was so angry last night I didn't even give her a chance to tell me what she wanted to say. I just assumed it was to do with her and de Brock. But when I accused her of having feelings for the man, she could not have feigned the shock she displayed to me. I can see that now, whereas last night I did not."

"What do you think she wanted to tell you?"

"I don't know. And now, I guess I never will."

Desmond struggled to his feet and reached beside his chair for a smooth stick he used to support his weight. "How do you know Melanie was not perchance going to tell you she was disturbed by the looks Dragon cast her way? Perhaps you were mistaken, Merick, when you thought she returned his admiration. Could it be she was frightened of the man?"

Merick pondered his brother's words for a moment. If she were frightened of de Brock, why then would she run away with him? It didn't make any sense. In fact, the more he mulled it over, the more preposterous the situation became. He had known Melanie her entire life. He knew her better than he knew himself. It was true she would be angered by his words last night. Actually, she would probably be enraged. But it wouldn't have driven her to run away with de Brock. Merick stood up suddenly, his brow becoming pinched with worry.

Desmond saw the change in his brother's visage and became concerned. "What ails you, Brother?"

"She would not have done it!"

"But you just said she would not have wanted to stay to face the public humiliation of having been put aside by you."

"Then she would have boxed my ears until they rang with reason. She would not have run off on her parents, or even on me, no matter what she was feeling."

Desmond's face paled. "Then that means...." He could not finish his thought.

Merick regarded him grimly. "It means Dragon has taken her."

~*~

"I say we take our complaint to the king and demand that Edward do something about this immediately!"

Lord de Balan looked at the man who had been his long-time friend and knew he was not thinking with reason. It was true the news of his daughter being snatched by de Brock had disturbed him greatly. Indeed, Fiona Worth had fainted after the announcement and had to be carried up to her room. Now, Alaine and Victor de Balan, Gordon Worth, and Merick paced the drawing room of Balan Castle. Desmond sat close by in a chair beside the hearth.

"You know Edward will not punish the man," Victor reminded him.

"Aye, he saved the Black Prince. The king owes him," agreed Desmond.

"Then how do we get her back?" Alaine demanded. She could not believe the nerve of de Brock. He came to their home to compete in a tournament, and not only did he hurt her precious son Desmond, but he also stole her soon to be daughter-in-law.

"We can put together an army the likes of which de Brock will not soon forget!" was Merick's suggestion. After he had concluded that Melanie was no willing companion of Dragon, he had quickly informed the others of what he knew.

The tournament games played on despite the absence of

the hosts. Victor and Alaine had opted to be discreet about what had happened to Melanie and not inform any of their guests. It had been difficult for Merick, but he had decided he would play on later this afternoon in the archery contest at his father's suggestion. There would be enough concern that Dragon had not stayed to compete in the tournament, and Merick did not want to add to the gossip. Tonight, though, after the games, there would be no betrothal announcement as they had planned. It was fortunate the de Balan's had kept it a secret so others would not wonder why there wasn't one.

Victor looked at his son and shook his head. "I am sorry, Merick. I know you would like nothing better than to ride in and tear down the walls of Tenebrous, but we cannot."

Merick looked sharply at his father. "Why can we not?"

"Because Tenebrous cannot be breached," Desmond answered for his father. "Even if it could, you would never make it out alive, even with a hundred men."

"De Brock has an undefeated fighting force, son."

"Surely, Father, they could not withstand the force of men you could put together," Merick insisted.

"Your father is unfortunately correct in his assessment, Merick," Alaine said, placing a comforting hand on her son's arm.

"De Brock's men are renowned for their fierceness, each of them handpicked and trained by the man himself. Only a fool would attempt to bring an army against him. You cannot get Melanie back by force, Merick," Desmond said. "And a siege would only enrage him and put Melanie at further risk."

Merick turned to Desmond. "Then tell me, Brother," he begged desperately. "Tell me how to get her back."

Desmond hesitated before he answered. He had an idea, but getting the others to agree to it would be difficult. "There might be a way," he began.

Merick knelt down before Desmond and grasped the arm of his chair. "Tell me. I'll do anything to bring her home."

"I propose we send a single man into the dragon's lair."

Desmond's suggestion was met with outrage from the small group. Before anyone could begin listing the reasons his plan was doomed for failure, Desmond banged his wooden stick upon the floor.

"Listen to me!" he yelled over the commotion. His outburst had the desired effect, and the room suddenly grew silent.

Desmond took a deep breath. "A single man could penetrate the walls of Tenebrous. Any more than that would arouse suspicion, considering de Brock is no doubt lying in wait for an attempt to get Melanie back. He would not, however, suspect a single man would dare attempt such a feat."

"By God, I think you may have something there, son," Victor said.

"It might work," allowed Gordon.

"But who shall go?" Alaine asked.

Merick had risen to his feet and walked toward the fire but turned at the sound of his mother's voice. "I shall go," he said quietly. When no one heard him, Merick repeated his words more forcefully. "I said, I shall go!"

Alaine smiled at her son indulgently. "Of course, you would, darling. But we must send someone that de Brock cannot identify."

"He might be able to right now, but in a few more days, he will not," Merick said, touching his bruised and swollen face.

"Son, it is understandable you would want to be the one, but you must know it cannot be so," Victor said.

"And why is that, Father? Could it be because I am not the

warrior Desmond is?"

Victor turned away from his son, afraid his expression would affirm his son's suspicion.

Alaine reached out to Merick, but he brushed her off as he marched across the room. He turned and faced the group, a determined look on his face.

"It must be me. Can you not see that?" Merick demanded. He had not told anyone other than Desmond what had transpired between him and Melanie, but the guilt he felt for his part in this calamity was overwhelming. If it had not been for his callous words, Melanie would never have gone off on her own. She would have been safe with him—at least a little safer, he thought, bitterly remembering how ineffective his protection had been at the pond. It dawned on Merick then that if de Brock had made the decision to have Melanie, nothing would have prevented him from taking her—especially not his feeble attempts to stop him. Nay, he would have succeeded at any cost.

Before the others could argue with Merick, Desmond spoke up in defense of his brother. "I think Merick is right." He put up his hand to forestall the inevitable arguments. "God forbid if anything has happened to Melanie, but if it has, she will not just go willingly with another man. She will trust no one but Merick."

Gordon Worth had a sick look upon his face. "I agree," he said quietly.

Victor let out a sigh as he looked at Merick. "All right, then. But we must come up with a plan."

The small group gathered around Desmond's chair, all thoughts now turned to crafting a foolproof plan to get Merick behind the walls of Tenebrous.

~*~

The stone wall was rough and cold against Melanie's back but still more desirable than the thought of sitting on the bed across from her. She had stared at that bed for over an hour, refusing to climb into it despite the discomfort she was in. When de Brock had first brought her to this high tower room, he had flung her onto that bed, and she had feared the worst. But he had only turned on his heel and retreated, locking the door behind him. She had not seen him since.

The ride to Tenebrous had been an arduous experience. At first, she did not know where it was de Brock planned to take her. When he had finally stopped hours later by the side of a stream to allow them a moment of rest, she had begged the information from him. He had been blunt with his explanation, saying only that he was taking her to his home. When she had asked what he wanted from her, thinking perchance he thought to ransom her, he had dashed that hope by saying he wanted her for marriage.

The announcement had stunned her.

The thought had been almost flattering — at first. Dragon had put a lot of thought and effort into securing her, even giving up much bounty from the tournament he was certain to win, but it was not because he so desired her to be his. Indeed, he had hardly spared her a glance since he took her, and when he did look at her, it was not with lust. Melanie had been confused by his treatment of her. He had seen to her comfort and safety during the day-and-a-half ride to Tenebrous, but his demeanor had been far from that of a love-struck man. If he wanted her for his wife, it was for another reason, but Melanie had not yet made sense of what it could be.

When they made camp and lain beneath the stars on the journey here, Melanie had thought de Brock might then make his move on her. She had held herself stiff and still when he put his blanket down close to hers beside the small fire. But instead of having to fend off his expected advances, he had rolled away from her and fallen asleep. Melanie had finally given in to her exhaustion when she heard de Brock begin to softly snore. His actions befuddled her greatly, for had his kiss in the forest not been an indication of his intent? Did he not desire her at all?

Melanie's fists clenched tightly as she remembered how she'd had to practically beg him for even the slightest bit of attention on their journey. It was true his thickly muscled arm had held her tightly round the waist as she sat before him on his horse, though she must admit he had only held her out of courtesy to keep her securely seated. She remembered the scent of him being intriguingly alluring, and the feel of his warm breath against her skin had made her quiver.

But he had not wanted her.

Perhaps he only wished to wait until they were wed, she soothed her bruised ego. She had seen the extent of his skill upon the field and assured herself that his restraint must be no less enduring. Melanie finally stood up and walked toward the bed with legs that shook in protest. Too long had she sat upon the cold stone floor pondering the intent of de Brock. One thing was certain in her mind, though, as she lay down and pulled the covers up to her chin. It was going to be one cold day in hell before she ever agreed to marry that man.

Chapter 7

Merick sat in a chair at his bedside, pulling on his boots. The sun was just beginning to rise, the glint of brightness peeking through the open window. He turned his face toward the light and determined that today would be the day. It had been four long days since de Brock had left Balan Castle with Melanie. Merick felt confident his face had healed enough to move ahead with Desmond's plan. Each night he had lain in his bed, a cold cloth draped across his face to help diminish the swelling. As he'd lain awake worrying about the fate of his beloved, he had risen many times throughout the night to soak the cloth when the coolness diminished. The fear that twisted his belly had not lessened as the color in his face slowly returned to normal. He could only hope he would not be recognized at Tenebrous. Desmond had assured him he could venture to Dragon's castle with a group of players and pass himself off as one of them. Then, once inside, he could find Melanie and hopefully make his escape unnoticed.

The plan sounded simple enough, but the fear Merick felt was palpable. What if he failed, he had endlessly worried?

If de Brock recognized him, despite the disguise he planned to wear, all would be lost. He would be killed, and Melanie would be sealed in her fate. There had been too many close calls in the past where his betrothed was concerned. Too many times when he had failed her by not being the man she had needed him to be. Why would this time be any different? he thought bitterly as he rose and walked toward the open window.

"Are you ready, Brother?"

Desmond stood crookedly at the doorway, leaning heavily on his crutch. Merick turned and regarded his older brother with a fearful glance.

"I must admit I am afraid."

Desmond moved closer until he stood before him. They were of the same height, and each looked the other in the eye. "You will not fail. Do not think having fear makes you a coward. It only makes you careful."

Merick smiled. "You are never afraid."

"That is why I am a fool." Desmond smiled ruefully, glancing down at his damaged leg.

Merick had packed a small sack the night before with a few necessities but nothing that would give away his true identity. The cloak he tossed over his shoulders was rough and worn. He lifted the sack from the trunk, holding it tightly against his chest like a shield.

"You are ready?" Desmond repeated.

"Aye. As ready as I will ever be."

The two left the room and headed downstairs toward the kitchen. None had risen yet, except a few servants who were milling about. Merick had wanted it this way. He'd said his goodbyes last night and had no wish to repeat assurances to his mother that all would be well. Cook had packed enough food for him and the others to see them through the journey to Tenebrous.

The brothers entered the courtyard, where a group of three men and two women awaited them. They were the troupe of players he would be traveling with, Merick hoping to pass himself off as one of them. For three days, the men and women had taught him their act, being well compensated for their direction. They had been inside the walls of Tenebrous once before and were certain they would have little problem gaining access again.

Merick grasped Desmond's arm in farewell. "Do not come for me, Brother. If I have not returned by summer's end, you will know I have failed."

Desmond had warned Merick this plan might not succeed as easily or as quickly as they hoped. If Merick could not rescue Melanie before the players were to leave the castle, it was going to be up to him to find a way to stay on. Finding Melanie might prove difficult, for Dragon could have hidden her away. Getting her out could be a strenuous task.

Merick gave his brother and Balan Castle one last look before he turned and began to walk toward the postern gate. The players followed along, giving him enough space to be alone with his thoughts.

At nightfall, they made camp by the edge of a stream. The group was a cheerful bunch despite the circumstance of their journey. Merick could not fault them for their behavior. Though they had no personal relationship with Melanie, they felt compassion for Merick's distress. They had withdrawn a respectable distance from the fire so they would not disturb him.

Beverly, one of the female players, stepped away from the rambunctious group and drew up alongside the fire to stand by Merick. He looked up at her from his seated position and beckoned her to join him. As she sat closely by his side, Merick turned his gaze back toward the flames.

Bevenly sat quietly, sensing Merick's sadness. She was startled when his deep voice finally broke the silence.

"It has been a long journey by foot. You must be weary?" he asked her.

She turned to him and felt mesmerized by the way the light of the fire caught his eyes and made them sparkle. "Aye, m'lord," she said simply, feeling slightly flushed over his concern. Traveling long distances by foot was not something new to her, but the heat had been scorching today, making the journey overly hard.

She had watched Merick as they walked. Being a player since the time she was eleven years of age had allowed her to meet a variety of people, both noble and baseborn. The nobles had considered her too beneath them to pay any mind to, except when she entertained them. But Merick had seemed different. He had not looked down on her and the others or treated them poorly. His kindness was evident, and Bevenly had been instantly besotted. She did not fool herself that there could ever be anything between them. Indeed, even now, they were off to rescue his ladylove. But perhaps he may need comfort, the kind she would be more than willing to offer him.

Merick could feel the young woman's gaze burning into him. If he were more like his brother, he would have no problem answering the obvious question she silently asked. But he was not Desmond. And the only woman he wanted, now and always, was Melanie. It was she who set his heart aflame and caused his blood to rush. Even now, wondering if she lay beneath Dragon, finally conquered by his raging lust, he still wanted her. Merick reached out to kindly pat Bevenly's hand. Then he rose and walked off to find his bed alone.

~*~

Melanie paced the hardwood floor of her room, occasionally pausing to climb up on a chair to peek out the high narrow window. By grasping the rough bars and craning her neck, she could make out the ground below. She heard a rider yelling out to have the gates opened, and Melanie hurried up onto the chair, hoping it was Dragon leaving Tenebrous. She might then finally cast off this charade of being in poor health and be allowed to leave this cursed tower. She climbed back down in defeat, for the man leaving was not nearly large enough to be de Brock.

For days she had rushed to curl up into a tight ball on her bed whenever anyone entered the room. She feared if she did not pretend to be sick, de Brock would try to make her his own. He had entered the room the second day she had been a prisoner here and demanded that she accompany him upon the dais for supper. When she had pleaded an upset stomach, he had gruffly told her to rest and then gone away. In the days since, she had eaten only very little from the trays of food brought to her room. She had eaten so little, in fact, that she had grown weak from lack of sustenance. But she was determined to continue the sham. And it had been successful, for de Brock had left her alone.

Melanie slumped onto her bed and lay down. She needed to conserve what little strength she had left so she would be ready to fight for her innocence. Certainly, it was only a matter of time before de Brock tired of her whining and would take her, willing or not.

The maid who had brought her trays of food was old, with gray hair pulled back tightly and covered with a kerchief. She did not say much to Melanie other than to ask how she was feeling. Although her words were few, her sad eyes had told Melanie plenty. They held such sympathy when they roamed over

Melanie's curled up form. Melanie knew the old woman feared for her, knowing that Dragon had brought the young maiden here and locked her away. And she knew what he intended to do to her. Her eyes told Melanie all of these things. And they also told her there was no hope, for who could save her from this fate?

The long hours spent alone gave her time to think. She thought mostly of Merick and the last time she had seen him. It had been that horrible night he had accused her of wanting de Brock. Melanie remembered the look on his face when he had released her from their betrothal. When he discovered her missing along with de Brock, she wondered if Merick had assumed she had left with him willingly. Would his anger cloud his judgment to the extent he would think her so desperate and foolish? Melanie didn't know what to think. Her head felt full of cobwebs, and her body felt so weak.

The door creaked open, and Melanie sat up quickly in the darkness. She must have drifted off to sleep, for the room had grown so dim. She sat back as far as she could and pulled the blanket up around her protectively. As her eyes peered at the large looming shadow coming forward, Melanie knew it was de Brock. His overbearing form made the room suddenly feel uncomfortably small. She feared this man. Though he had been nothing but patient and distant with her, even showing slight compassion for her discomfort, she did not trust him in the slightest. He had made his intentions toward her clear with his blunt announcement on their ride to Tenebrous. He meant to wed her, and Melanie had no idea how to stop that from happening. Before she could utter a word, de Brock stepped aside to reveal that he was not alone. A young maid had been behind him, hidden by his great size.

"See to her," de Brock demanded before he turned on his

heel and strode from the room, slamming the door behind him.

The maid came forward and cautiously approached Melanie's bedside. She held in her hands a tray laden with what looked to be medicinal supplies. She set the tray gently down on the table by the bed and looked kindly at Melanie.

"I am here to ease your pain, my lady," she said.

Melanie regarded the young woman cautiously. She was small in stature like herself and looked to be of the same age. Though a kerchief covered the top of her head, a thick mane of long brown locks cascaded down her back. Her eyes were a soft brown filled with compassion, and Melanie felt herself drawn to her.

"It is not so bad right now," Melanie admitted, but then looked at the maid with sudden trepidation, for what if her compassion had been feigned?

"Fear not, my lady. I will not betray you to my lord."

Melanie relaxed her grip on the bed sheets with relief. She smiled back at the maid. Perhaps she could befriend her. She did not seem to fear de Brock like the old woman that brought her meals.

"My name is Kallie, my lady."

"It is a pleasure to meet you, Kallie. Although, I do wish the circumstances were different. I am Melanie." Melanie climbed off the bed and gestured for Kallie to sit in one of the two chairs. Kallie sat down while Melanie began to pace the confines of the small room.

"You're probably wondering how it is that I came to be locked away in your lord's tower."

"It is not my place to wonder about such things, my lady. I was only told to aid you in your recovery."

"You do know why it is your lord wishes me well, do you

not? It is so he can force me into marriage," Melanie spat.

Kallie looked at Melanie with pity. "I know Lord de Brock must make a good match, for he is in desperate need of funds."

Melanie stopped pacing. "He what!"

"I am sorry to tell you this, my lady, but if you think he brought you here out of love, you are mistaken. It is only coin he desires."

"That dirty rotten brute! That explains why he kissed me with such passion at Balan Castle and then treated me so callously on the ride here—he was only sampling the goods!"

"He kissed you?" Kallie gasped, rising from her chair.

"Y...yes." Melanie was confused by the maid's sudden change in demeanor, although when Kallie took her seat, she was again composed.

"Do not fear, my lady. I shall do my best to aid you."

"I do not wish to wed him, but I don't know how much longer I can put him off," Melanie admitted.

"I have a few ideas which may help you in that regard," Kallie assured her.

Melanie, intrigued by the determined look on the maid's face, sat in the other chair and listened to Kallie's plan.

~*~

Merick and his traveling companions finally arrived within the last league of their destination. They had crested a hill that overlooked Castle Tenebrous from a distance, gaining them an unhampered view of the fortress. The brush helped to obscure their arrival from Dragon's diligent watchmen and allowed the weary group to gaze below unchallenged.

After staring at Tenebrous for several moments, Merick looked behind him at the players he had come to know over the past few days. He was surprised to discover how fond he had grown of the rag-tag group who had put their own lives on hold in order to aid him in his quest. The easiest part of the journey was over, and now came the moment of truth. Even if they gained entrance to the castle, there would be no guarantee things would end the way Merick desired. He had lain awake last night staring at the stars in the sky, his belly knotted with dread, fearing he had come too late to save Melanie.

Bevenly smiled at him, and Merick took strength in her unwavering faith in him.

"Friends," he began, gaining the attention of his companions. "We have arrived, but I fear, now that the moment is upon us, I cannot ask you to risk your lives in this endeavor. It may be we will gain admittance to the dragon's lair, but I cannot guarantee your safe return." Merick paused before continuing his speech. "Any promises you have given to myself or my brother, I consider fulfilled. You may venture forth on your own path, for I would not forgive myself if I have led you astray."

The players' faces showed their obvious confusion over Merick's words. They tittered momentarily amongst themselves before Tol stepped forward to speak for the group.

"My lord, we have not come this far to just leave you at the gates. We gave our word we would get you inside Tenebrous, and that is what we intend to do. Let us go and get your lady."

Merick smiled gratefully at all of them and openly laughed as they crowded around him, taking turns to grasp his arm in the bond of friendship. The girls were less inhibited and hugged him tightly to their breasts.

"Onward then!" Merick said, and began to descend the hill in the direction of the castle.

They'd barely reached the bottom when a large, vicious group of riders suddenly broke from the surrounding forest and rode toward Tenebrous. Merick and the players froze and watched, horrified as the gates of the castle suddenly flung wide and a band of soldiers, dressed all in black and red, charged out to meet their opponents.

Merick quickly heralded his group toward the edge of the forest to keep them safely from the fray. He could clearly see de Brock's men were outnumbered at least three to one, but this did not stop them from riding ahead at full speed. The clash shook the ground as swords met in a dance of death. The prowess of Dragon's men stunned the observers, and they gaped over the lightning agility of the men. These were men accustomed to battle. Blood lust coursed through their hardened bodies as they quickly and ruthlessly dispatched their enemies. The attackers soon realized the futility of their assault and began to disband. Scattering in four directions, they strove to escape the soldiers, who split up and rode after them.

Merick and the players watched fearfully as a group of riders suddenly aimed their horses in their direction. The two women screamed and ran into the forest for cover. The men followed, but not soon enough to elude the riders who cut them down as they flew past. Merick leaped behind a thick rotten tree trunk that lay on the forest floor and ducked his head to keep from sight. He no longer feared the men who had attacked Tenebrous, for they had ridden on. It was now de Brock's soldiers he hid from.

But then he heard screams of agony from the formidable Tenebrous soldiers. Merick peeked out to see what could have befallen such powerful men. He was amazed to see arrows flying out from the trees along the faint trail the men followed. Merick then realized they had been led into a trap. At least three of de Brock's men lay dead or wounded upon the forest floor. Two others rode their horses in circles around them, unwilling to leave, but wary of the arrows that continued to rain down from above. Merick felt the ground beneath him shake from the thundering of horses' hooves and feared the attackers had turned around and would soon resume their assault. From his position, he faintly made out a man crouching in a tree firing arrows from his bow.

Merick knew he must make a stand. He rolled silently to a crouch and reached beneath his cape for his own quiver of arrows. He pulled forth his bow and set an arrow in place, aimed, and released, hitting his mark square on. The man fell to the ground below, landing with a sickening thump. The death of a comrade momentarily stopped the deadly attack from above, but when it resumed, Merick was ready. He had already moved into position to spot another man balancing in a tree above.

Merick saw his chance and took it.

He again aimed and felled the man with a single shot. Three more arrows flew with deadly accuracy, and three more men fell from above to lie dead upon the forest floor. And then there was only silence. The riders who had been approaching must have caught sight of their fallen fellows and quickly turned their horses back the way they had come. The remaining Tenebrous soldiers began to give chase but soon returned when they were certain the men had left for good.

Merick wiped the sweat from his brow as he looked at the bodies he had brought low. The threat from these men was no longer tangible, but as Merick raised his glance to the horse and rider who had suddenly appeared before him, he knew a moment of dread. For there before him was one of Dragon's men, and the look upon his face was not of one who welcomed Merick's intrusion.

Chapter 8

Jamie de Brock sat at the dais, waiting for the evening meal to be served. He was growing concerned, for he had expected Melanie to join him at the table tonight, but it seemed it was not to be so. He had known the girl would deny him her company when she first arrived — the excuses she made to remain in the tower were expected. But then, he had begun to think it might be more than just her fear of him that kept her confined to her bed. He looked at Kallie anxiously as she approached the high board, not bothering to mask his interest.

"My lord, I bring you news of Lady Melanie," she said.

"What ails her?"

Kallie leaned closely toward Jamie so the others seated nearby would not overhear her voice. "It is as I thought, my lord when you first approached me and described her symptoms."

"She is afraid," Jamie interrupted impatiently.

"Nay, my lord. It is not fear that knots her belly. It is only her woman's time."

Jamie dragged a hand through his thick mane of hair in

a gesture of habit. "Oh. All right. She should be ready to come below soon then?"

Kallie smiled at him, which only increased his sudden discomfort. "A few days, my lord," she assured him.

"Did you give her something? To ease the pain, I mean."

Kallie cocked an eyebrow at him. "Aye. It is kind of you to feel such concern for Lady Melanie."

"You know why that is," Jamie reminded her. When Kallie smiled tightly at him, he quickly became interested in the trencher sitting before him. He looked up a moment later, hoping Kallie had gone back to the kitchen, but she still remained. When he regarded her questioningly, she put her hands on her hips in frustration. Jamie then realized he had neglected to give her permission to go. He gave her a quick nod of his head in dismissal and watched her turn on her heel and stalk back across the room.

"Women," he grumbled, wondering if he would ever get used to having females in his castle.

The meal was nearing completion when the doors to the great hall suddenly burst open. Jamie had been expecting this interruption, for he had seen a group of his men ride out earlier to clash with Fontleroy's soldiers. He had almost come to expect their weekly barrage now, for it seemed they were determined to draw him out to battle with them openly. It had galled Lord Fontleroy tremendously that the legendary Dragon considered Fontleroy too beneath him to fight him man to man. Fontleroy figured if he caused enough of these little skirmishes, he would eventually anger Jamie enough to meet him on the field.

Since Jamie had returned to England from fighting for Edward, he had met up with man after man who wished to challenge him. Besides gaining Tenebrous Castle for his exploits in France, he'd also gained a fierce reputation. Jamie did not care

how many times the fool Fontleroy bothered to charge his gates —
he was tired of always having to prove himself. He had a castle to
run. He couldn't take time to ride out to fight every knight who
showed up at the gates for a challenge. The men from Hatchel
castle provided distraction as well as sport to Jamie's men who
had never viewed them as a threat. As long as none of Jamie's
men were hurt, he was content to let them have their fun.

Tristan, Jamie's man, came forward, followed by Holden.
The men were bloodied and looked at Jamie anxiously. Jamie got
to his feet at once, knowing something serious had happened.

"My lord," began Tristan. "Fontleroy's soldiers have taken
the game beyond the boundaries of their usual play."

"What happened?" demanded Jamie.

"We were ambushed, my lord," Holden said.

"Ambushed! By a bunch of untrained fools?"

Tristan looked at Jamie angrily. "Aye! The dogs split off,
and we gave chase. Three of our men have fallen."

"Three!" Jamie growled.

Hearing the anger from their lord, others around the room
left their tables and gathered around the high table.

"We were attacked from above, my lord! They fled into
the woods, and as we followed, arrows rained from the trees
overhead," Holden explained.

"We'd have all been injured or worse if Fontleroy's men
hadn't been stopped by a man in the forest."

"A man? What man? How did he stop them?" Jamie asked.

"We do not know who he is. We hadn't time to question
him, my lord. We brought him in with us, and he is now under
guard outside the great hall," Holden said.

"He killed every man in the trees by felling them with
his bow and arrow," Tristan told him, his voice edged with the

disbelief he still felt over the feat.

"My men—the three brought low by the arrows. How do they fare?" Jamie asked.

"Alive, my lord. Even now, they are with the physician who tends them. They will survive, but it would have been a different tale if it had not been for that man."

"Bring him to me," Jamie said, his voice cold and unreadable as he retook his seat.

Holden strode toward the doors of the hall and leaned out to gesture for the men to bring forth the stranger. Merick, flanked by two soldiers, soon stood before Jamie.

Jamie eyed him thoughtfully for a long moment before he spoke. "Who are you?" he asked.

Merick began to speak but had to stop to clear his throat. "I...I am Reginald Fenlay, my lord," he replied. Merick held his hands clasped tightly before him, worried the tremors running through him would betray his deceit.

"And what were you doing sneaking around in my forest?" Jamie demanded.

"My lord," Merick began, despising the sweat he felt running down his back. "We had only arrived when we were suddenly caught in the clash between your men and the attackers."

"We?"

"Aye, my lord. A small group and I of players come to seek admittance to Tenebrous."

"And where are the others?" Jamie asked suspiciously.

A shadow crossed Merick's face as he began to feel the pain of despair. Caught up in all the chaos of the past hour, he had not given thought to his fellow comrades. The guilt washing over him now almost brought him to his knees.

"I saw the women flee into the forest as the attackers

approached," he began, his voice no more than a whisper. "The men and I stood our ground until the women were safely away. We also meant to escape, but we were too late. As the riders passed, they struck at us with their swords. I took cover, but I saw my friends fall. Whether they be alive or dead, I know not, my lord."

Jamie saw the uncertainty cross the man's face when he had asked him the question. There could be no disguising the agony he had suddenly felt. Jamie looked at Tristan, his look questioning him as to the fate of the male players. Tristan gave a slight shake of his head, telling his lord that the men hadn't survived. Though Jamie saw the distress of the man before him, he could not allow it to sway him. "How is it that a mere player displays such skill with a bow?"

Merick squeezed his hands together tightly as he prepared to explain himself with his practiced lie. "It is part of our act, my lord. I can shoot an apple from atop a man's head. Quite a popular request." Merick's smile didn't quite reach his eyes.

Jamie sighed and leaned back in his chair. It was clear to him the man standing before him had no idea what it was he'd done. Single-handedly he had saved the lives of three of Jamie's warriors while losing three of his own friends. Jamie owed this man a debt of thanks. A debt that he knew must be honored.

"You will remain at Tenebrous as my guest," Jamie told him, his statement more of a demand than a request.

Merick breathed a sigh of relief. It had worked! His story and disguise had fooled the mighty Dragon! He should want to jump for joy. For now, he could remain and seek out Melanie just as he had planned. But he did not feel like celebrating. Instead, as he thought of his friends, the men who had given their very lives for this quest, and the women, whose fate was still unknown, he felt a heaviness in his chest.

"My lord, I will accept your most gracious offer. I have been through much this afternoon, and I would ask if there may be a quiet alcove where I may rest awhile."

Jamie inclined his head to his guest. "But of course. Tristan will see to your comfort." Jamie instructed his man to take the player to the second floor of Tenebrous and set him up in one of the small chambers used for guests.

Merick overheard Jamie's words and felt slightly awkward at de Brock's charity. Before Tristan led him away, Merick almost told his host that he would be just as comfortable bunking with the other men. He did not wish to draw unwanted attention to his presence but then decided that seclusion might better serve his purpose. Tristan led him out of the hall and past the entranceway of the castle where Merick had been held while waiting to see de Brock. They climbed a narrow staircase set strategically against the right side of the wall. If attackers ever gained entrance to the castle, they would be forced to carry their sword in their left hand while they climbed the stairs, giving an advantage to the castle inhabitants. Desmond had warned Merick, however, that Dragon and his men needed no such benefit, for they were highly skilled in the use of both of their hands in combat.

Tristan led Merick down a wide hallway, and with each doorway they passed, Merick strained his ears, hoping to hear his beloved's voice. He knew there were three more floors above and then four towers, one in each corner of the castle, which could also imprison Melanie. It could take days, he knew, for him to search the castle for her. He only required time and a great deal of luck.

They stopped at the end of the hall, and Tristan opened the door and stepped into the room before them. "It is small, I'm afraid but comfortable. I'll send someone up with food."

"My thanks, that would be much appreciated," Merick said.

Tristan smiled then and reached out to put a friendly hand on Merick's shoulder. "One of the men you saved today…he was my younger brother. If you have need of anything, anything at all, simply ask, and it shall be yours."

Merick smiled tightly, declining to speak, for all he wished for was the safe return of Melanie, but he doubted it was something Tristan was willing to grant him.

~*~

Melanie was pacing the confines of the east tower when she heard the door to her room being unlocked. She felt a moment of trepidation until she saw Kallie step within. Melanie waited patiently as she watched the maid place a tray on the table and uncover her meal.

"What has happened?" Melanie asked, anxious to know what was going on below.

"My lord understands you are unwell and not willing to join him at the table. I assured him the condition that plagues you is only temporary, and you should be well enough to come down in a few days," Kallie said.

Melanie cringed over the maid's words, knowing they would have to come up with another excuse as to why she was avoiding company with de Brock. Though she had been wondering what de Brock's reaction would be with Kallie's prognosis, the anxiousness she felt was for another reason. She had seen from her window that the castle had been under attack. For a moment, she had prayed it had been an army of soldiers from Balan Castle come to rescue her. She had envisioned Merick leading the men into battle, sitting high atop his horse, charging toward the gates of Tenebrous, sword waving angrily in the air. Overcoming his fears so he may save her from the clutches of the evil Dragon.

But then she had seen the Tenebrous soldiers ride out to meet the invaders. Though outnumbered, they had easily driven back the opposing riders and scattered them in four different directions before giving chase. She had no longer thought the riders had come for her after getting a better look at the garb they wore. Balan's soldiers wore the colors of blue and gold with the crest of a falcon clearly displayed upon their chest. These soldiers had been dressed all in green, whereas Dragon's men wore black and red with a dragon emblazoned on their surcoats.

Hopes dashed. Melanie had watched as the land before the castle had grown silent. It had been a long while before she saw some of the soldiers return to regroup in front of the castle before riding off in the direction of the forest to join their comrades.

She saw them exit the forest several minutes later, and to her horror, saw several bodies thrown over the backs of the soldiers' mounts. If the men they carried were alive or dead, she did not know. A single man was on foot, and Melanie had seen his hands were tied before him, the rope held by a Tenebrous soldier riding beside him. She had noticed the man was dressed colorfully but poorly, resembling the players she had recently seen at Balan Castle. Her eyes had strained to see the man's face. Something about him had seemed vaguely familiar even from the distance separating them. Perhaps it had been the way he carried his body, shoulders hunched, his head hanging in defeat, trying to appear small despite his obvious height. It was a stance Merick had often assumed when coming under the scrutiny of his assailants. He had thought if he made himself appear small and non-threatening, the bullies would leave him alone.

"I have brought you something to eat," Kallie said, pulling a chair up to the table.

"I am not hungry," Melanie said. "Kallie, tell me what has happened below, and I do not inquire as to the lord's reaction to my absence."

"Did you see the clash from your window then?" Kallie asked. She was hoping Melanie had not. It would have spared her a lengthy explanation, as she was needed below to help tend to the men who had been injured. If it had not been for Jamie's specific instruction to her that none should care for Melanie but herself, she would have sent Lilith with the lady's supper. But the old woman had carried on so about the climb to the tower that Jamie had assigned her duties to Kallie. Lilith also had expressed her fear of Melanie's condition, which reinforced Jamie's resolve that Melanie needed a skilled healer to care for her. Kallie had taken on the added burden of caregiver despite her misgivings of the task.

"Aye, I saw the men riding forth to attack Tenebrous." Still uncertain of the recent friendship with the maid, Melanie kept her earlier thoughts about the riders possibly being there to rescue her to herself.

"Fear not, for Lord de Brock's men rode out to meet the men and drive them off."

"I saw them. Who were the attackers?" Melanie asked.

Kallie hesitated slightly before revealing the name, unsure of how much she should tell the already frightened lady. "A few miles north of Tenebrous is Castle Hatchel, home of Lord Fontleroy, my lord's antagonist. I call him such, for he is ever attacking Tenebrous in the hopes of drawing out the legendary Dragon. He seeks to provoke my lord to do battle with him."

"He willingly seeks to fight de Brock?" Melanie gasped.

"Surely, the man must be mad."

Kallie smiled over the look on Melanie's face, experiencing a moment of pride in her lord's legendary prowess. "Either that or a fool, I think."

"Was it he who I saw then, being led back to the castle with his hands tied?"

"I know the man was not Lord Fontleroy, for he was dressed as a player. I only saw him briefly outside the great hall when I was summoned to help aid the men who had been injured."

"I saw the bodies being carried out of the forest," Melanie told her. Though she was being held here against her will, she did not wish ill against the men who served de Brock.

"Three of my lord's men were felled by arrows from attackers who had lain in wait for them in the trees. They had apparently been led into an ambush."

"How terrible!"

"Aye, but though painful, their wounds were superficial — they shall survive. The attackers that did not escape, however, were all killed."

"All of them killed?" Melanie asked, wondering who that man had been, if not one of the attackers.

"Shot out from the very trees they perched in, believe it or not — by the player!" Kallie revealed though she had hardly believed the news herself when Holden told her.

"A player displayed such skill?" Melanie asked in disbelief.

"Aye. He was being questioned by Lord de Brock while I was on my way up here with your supper," Kallie said.

"Does Lord de Brock think he's a spy then?"

"I do not think so, but I cannot be certain."

Melanie sat down at the little table. "Tell me what the man

looks like," she said, a hint of hope began to stir to life in her again.

Kallie regarded her curiously. "Why, do you think you may know him?" she asked.

"No," Melanie assured her quickly. "It is only that his garb resembled something similar to the players I had seen at Balan Castle. It is strange, though, that he would be traveling alone."

"He was not alone," Kallie said sadly. "Three of his fellows were brought in dead. Killed by Fontleroy's soldiers."

"Oh," Melanie said.

"Well, he was tall—very tall, and handsome too. Dark hair. I didn't see the color of his eyes, for his gaze was fastened on the floor. He had a slim build, obviously not a warrior. Strangely enough, although he was dressed poorly, he did not seem to be a peasant."

"Really?" Melanie asked, trying to keep the excitement from her voice.

"It is hard to describe, but there was an air about him. Perhaps it was the way he held himself. Though very frightened, he still seemed to carry himself as a nobleman. It was not overly apparent, but he wiped the sweat from his face with a cloth he had clumsily retrieved from his belt with his tied hands. It did not seem like something a peasant would do." Kallie shrugged her shoulders, and seeing the lady was now appearing to take an interest in her supper, she bid Melanie a good eve and left the chamber.

Melanie smiled secretly to herself. The gesture Kallie had described was something she had been very familiar with, for she had seen Merick do it a number of times. And though she could not be completely sure until she saw the man again, she felt certain that her love had come for her at last.

Chapter 9

Merick hesitated momentarily at the stairway before beginning the descent to the hall. He was tempted to ascend to the floors above and search for Melanie. It was still quiet in the castle, as the hour was early. He had risen before the sun, unable to sleep any longer. As it was, his night had passed far too slowly, and he had woken several times, being uneasy with his unfamiliar surroundings. His anxiousness about the task before him had made his stomach unsettled, and he'd had difficulty eating the supper brought to his room. The thought of his sweet Melanie, somewhere within these walls, had almost driven him mad with desperation to find her. He had stared at his door several times and even opened it once, only to find a guard posted down the hallway. The man had turned his head in Merick's direction and asked him if he required anything. Merick had replied that all was well, that he'd thought he'd heard a noise. He wasn't sure if the guard had been posted on the second floor as routine or if his presence was an added precaution, although he was not there this morning. Merick could not blame de Brock if the guard had been there to watch him. He, too, would be wary of a stranger who had exhibited deadly skill with a bow.

As Merick opened the doors to the great hall and stepped within, he could see Dragon was already seated upon the dais breaking his fast. He walked stiffly to keep his legs from shaking when Dragon saw him and motioned for him to come forward.

"Did you rest well?" Dragon inquired. A trencher of bread with roasted pork and several eggs sat before him.

"Very well," Merick lied. The tantalizing smell of the food from the table almost tempted his empty stomach. Dragon gestured for him to take a seat at one of the trestle tables. Though Merick felt a little strange breaking bread with his enemies, he did as he was bid and seated himself.

"My thanks," Merick said to Kallie as she set the tray before him.

"It is an honor to serve the man who has saved the lives of so many," Kallie told him, then left the table after exchanging a nod with her lord.

Merick ate slowly, unexpectedly enjoying the food. He was aware of the many stares he received and would have felt uncomfortable at the scrutiny if not for the kindness behind the looks. He could hear the men in the hall talking about his extraordinary feat yesterday, and he noted with surprise they regarded him as a hero. It was an unfamiliar feeling for him to be regarded as such, for that right had always been reserved for Desmond. Merick felt humbled by the experience and then undeserving when the faces of his fellow players flashed through his mind.

After the meal, Merick left the hall and went out to walk the grounds of Tenebrous. At first, he worried his presence might be challenged, but he grew bolder when it was apparent no one was going to stop him. He needed to familiarize himself with the lay of the land and then with the castle's interior if he hoped to plan his and Melanie's escape. Merick tilted his head back to look up at the towers of Tenebrous, wondering if his love might even now be looking down upon him.

From above, Melanie stood on the edge of a chair, peering down at what looked to be Merick's likeness just below her window. She could not believe her eyes. Seeing him come into view a short while ago, she'd watched him walk around the grounds. As he came closer to her tower and tilted back his head, it appeared he looked right at her. Though she felt certain it was Merick, she dared not call out to him for fear she would cause him harm. It was most certain he'd come to Tenebrous disguised as a player to rescue her. It was fate he'd come just as the castle had been under attack. Kallie had said it was a most usual occurrence. But what luck for Merick to have arrived and then saved some of Dragon's own men. Surely Merick would be looked upon with high regard at Tenebrous. It must be why he was allowed the freedom to walk the grounds.

Melanie noticed Merick stood alone. She knew she risked much, but she jumped down from the chair and tore a piece of her dress along the hem. She tied the piece around a short stick of wood from the hearth to lend it some weight, then climbed back on the chair and leaned out to stare at the grounds once again. Merick was still there. Melanie shoved the piece of wood and cloth through the bars of the window and watched it fall to the ground. Thankfully, he saw her offering, but no one else had noticed. Merick leaned down to pick it up. He untied the wood from the cloth and dropped the wood to the ground. She saw him lift the cloth to his nose and inhale her scent. Melanie felt a tear slip down her face when Merick brushed the cloth against his cheek.

A sudden flurry of activity before the gates of Tenebrous caught Melanie's attention. She could see from her view that five of Dragon's men were entering within. One of the men had a woman seated on his mount before him. Melanie noticed the woman was barely staying upright in the saddle. The only thing keeping her steady was the support of the man's arm wrapped around her waist. When Melanie looked back down toward Merick, she saw his attention was now riveted on the men riding into the yard. Merick looked up at the tower, tucked the piece of cloth into his shirt, and turned and walked toward the men.

Melanie watched him go. It took all her restraint not to scream out to him at the top of her lungs. She had so much to tell him! These dark days spent isolated in the tower had given her much time to think. She wanted to say she loved him just as he was. After a taste of being subjected to the whims of a mighty warrior, she'd come to realize how much Merick's sweetness meant to her. Regret filled her for taking him for granted. All their moments together she had wasted. She'd been filled with longing of how she'd wanted him to be different, when all along, he'd been exactly what she needed.

The woman on the horse was lowered into waiting arms. Merick worked his way through the small crowd forming in the yard until he could see Dragon's men and the woman. He gasped in surprise and then cried out in joy. "Bevenly!" Quickly he stepped forward to take her from the man who held her.

As Merick knelt upon the ground with Bevenly in his arms, the soldier regarded him. Tristan was amongst the men, and he looked at Merick. "Do you know this woman, Reginald?" he asked him.

Merick did not respond to the question, forgetting

momentarily he had given the false name as his own.

"Reginald?" Tristan repeated.

This time, Merick, remembering himself, turned his gaze to him. "Aye, I know her. She is a fellow player." He turned his attention back to Bevenly. "Bevenly, can you hear me?"

Bevenly roused slightly at the sound of Merick's voice. She opened her eyes and struggled against his arms.

"Do not be afraid, Bevenly. 'Tis I, Reginald," Merick said, praying the shaken woman would remember the ruse and not betray his true identity.

Bevenly's eyes finally focused fully upon Merick, and she relaxed her struggles. "Reginald," she whispered, her voice hoarse and uncertain.

Merick breathed a sigh of relief. "It is I." He lifted her gently from his lap to place her on the ground and got slowly to his feet. "Can you stand?" he asked her, offering his hand.

Bevenly put her hand in his. "I think so."

Merick raised her up and put a firm arm around her waist to keep her steady. "What happened to you?" he asked, distressed by her disheveled appearance. Except for some scrapes and scratches, a good amount of dirt, and some slight bruising, she did not appear to be hurt.

Bevenly looked around, fearfully regarding all the unfamiliar faces. The soldiers had surrounded the pair, still uncertain what to make of the woman.

"I ran into the forest when I saw the riders approaching us," she began. "I was alone. Annette and I became separated as we ran. After a distance, I hid. Though I could still hear sounds of battle, I felt safe enough where I was. I was overly cautious and did not try to make my way out of the forest for a long while. As I walked back the way I had come, I saw...."

Merick saw the look of horror cross her face, and his grip tightened protectively around her. "What did you see, Bevenly?" he asked gently.

"'Twas Annette. She was dead. A bloody wound ran down the length of her chest."

"Jesu…," Merick breathed.

"I was so frightened, I just began running. By the time I stopped, I was lost. I could not find my way back out of the forest, and I had to spend the night on the ground. In the morning, I again tried to get back to the edge of the woods. That was when they found me," she said, looking at Tristan and the others.

"You are safe now," Merick assured her. "No one will harm you here."

Tristan looked around at the group of onlookers still gathered in the yard. "Get back to work now, all of you," he yelled. The people dispersed slowly, still wanting to get a look at the woman being held by the man who had become a legend overnight.

"I want you to come inside Tenebrous," Tristan said to Bevenly. "Reginald can help you. I would like to have our physician tend your wounds."

The other soldiers walked on ahead, leading their mounts to the stables, while Tristan led Merick and Bevenly into the castle. Inside, he brought them to a small room at the rear of the first floor. He opened the door and walked within, not bothering to knock. Merick entered behind him, followed by Bevenly. Inside were four cots, three of which still held the soldiers that were hurt in the ambush yesterday. All three of the men appeared to be resting comfortably, their wounds bandaged capably. A man who looked to be in his fiftieth year was bent over a table covered with instruments, bandages, and vials of medicines, their strong scents filling the air.

"I have another patient for you, Canhem," Tristan said.

The older man looked up from the table and peered at the trio. "Have you, now?" he asked, turning his attention to Bevonly. He took her arm and gently led her to the vacant bed. "Do not worry about these young fellows," he said, gesturing at his other patients and giving her a wink. "They won't be capable of doing much of anything for some time yet."

Bevonly smiled, her tenseness slowly easing with the kind man's banter. Canhem returned to his table to fetch a clean cloth and a bowl of water to wash the dirt and grime from Bevonly's cuts. As he went about his work, Tristan knelt at the beside of a young man who lay on a cot. He gestured for Merick to join him, and Merick walked over hesitantly.

"Benton, I want you to meet the man who saved your life," Tristan said.

Benton awkwardly pulled himself into a sitting position with the help of Tristan and reached out his hand to clasp Merick's. "'Tis a pleasure, sir."

"I am glad you are well," Merick said. He didn't have to be told this was Tristan's brother. The young man's shoulder-length blond hair and fair looks greatly resembled his older sibling's.

"Is it true you shot five men from the trees with your bow?" Benton asked.

"I assure you it is true," came a deep voice from the doorway.

"My lord!" All the men in the room spoke at once to greet their lord, Jamie de Brock.

Jamie strode toward Tristan and Merick and looked down kindly at Benton. "You are looking well."

"Aye, my lord."

"Then I expect to see you out on the training field by week's end," Jamie said. Benton groaned, as did the other men, knowing the same would be expected of them. "I was told we had another player in our midst," Jamie said to Tristan.

"Aye, we found her this morning by the edge of the forest."

Jamie looked over at the woman and noticed she was regarding him fearfully. He gave her a brief nod to try and ease her distress, but it did not seem to have the desired effect.

Merick saw the exchange and tried to explain Bevenly's trepidation. "She has been through much, my lord. She came across the body of another woman who was part of our troupe."

"A shame," Jamie said. "But at least this one survived."

"Aye," Merick readily agreed.

A flash of anger crossed Jamie's brow momentarily. "Damn Fontleroy and his foolish pranks. I fear I am to be forever plagued by that man's presence."

"Fontleroy?" Merick asked.

"My neighbor hails from Hatchel Castle. The fool attempts to draw me out to engage in battle," Jamie explained.

"'Tis almost a weekly occurrence now," Tristan said. "He was amusing with his vain and pathetic attacks, though this time he has gone too far!"

Jamie knew how close Tristan had come to losing the only remaining member of his family, and he realized the man was right. He had let things with Fontleroy go on far too long. He couldn't help but feel responsible as he looked around the room at his wounded men — men that might have perished if not for the player and his timely rescue. Men had been killed this time, though they'd not been his soldiers, and a woman as well. Jamie could imagine the anger that must be coursing through the player's veins. It seemed they now shared a common bond, and

Jamie wondered if the player's need for vengeance might be as strong as his own.

"I will bid you farewell, for there are plans to be made. Walk with me, player," Jamie said, nodding his head in the direction of the doorway.

"Farewell," the men echoed.

Merick cast a smile to Bevenly, who was watching him with frightened eyes, then he bid farewell to Tristan and the others. "Good day to you," the men in the room said to Merick as he left to join Dragon.

~*~

Melanie was pacing the tower room fretfully when she heard the key to her door being turned. She tried to calm herself so that she would not appear apprehensive to Kallie, who would be returning to fetch her tray from breakfast. She liked Kallie, but it was too soon to trust her with Merick's fate. One word from Kallie, and all could be lost.

"Did you see?" Kallie asked breathlessly.

"See what?" Though desperate to inquire about the fate of the woman who'd been brought within the gates, she dare not seem too anxious.

"Another player was found. The men just brought her in."

"Alive?" Melanie questioned, remembering how the woman had been slumped over in the saddle. She hadn't seen her again, for the crowd had been too thick.

"Aye, she's been taken to the physician."

For a moment, Melanie felt afraid, for if this woman was one of the players who had traveled with Merick, then she surely must be in on his ruse. What if the woman, in her distressed state, unintentionally revealed Merick's true identity?

"How does she fare?" Melanie asked, careful to keep her

voice steady.

"I do not know. I will inquire when I am again below, for I must aid the physician. The sick room is quite overflowing with patients."

"Oh," Melanie said, turning away to hide her disappointment.

Kallie walked up to the table and picked up the half-eaten tray of food. "You do not have to pretend to be ill any longer," she informed Melanie. "Besides, it is now past the time that your flux would be ended."

"But Lord de Brock will want me to join him below," Melanie said fearfully.

Kallie looked at her pointedly. "You know you cannot remain in this room forever."

"I do not intend to," Melanie said quickly, then bit her lip.

Kallie smiled. "I know you continue to hold out hope someone will rescue you, but I assure you, that will not happen. It is just not possible."

Melanie felt a chill run over her. Kallie spoke so assuredly, as though she knew without a doubt any attempt to save her would be in vain. "Surely Tenebrous is not unbreachable," Melanie said, and laughed lightly.

"I know if anyone attempted to gain entrance here by force or trickery, it would be their death."

Melanie pretended to become interested in one of the threads from her tattered dress. Her expression would no doubt betray her anguish over Kallie's announcement. "Perhaps I could gain the trust of Dragon and escape him then?"

Kallie frowned at Melanie's words. "Surely you would not attempt to do something so foolish, my lady. I do not mean to frighten you, but I must stress how serious your situation is. Aye, you may one day escape my lord, but you must think hard about what it is you attempt to do. The threats you face are not only at Tenebrous," Kallie reminded her.

"What do you mean?" Melanie asked.

"Do you so soon forget what you witnessed the other day? Lord Fontleroy is beyond the walls, just waiting for a chance to draw out my lord. He would not think twice of capturing you and using you to gain power over my lord. Too, if you do get past Fontleroy, there is still a long journey to your home. The road is rife with desperate men, and the forest is full of dangerous animals. How will you find substance? Where will you sleep? Are you certain you know the direction home? What if you became lost?"

Melanie suddenly felt ill for real. She sat down hard on the bed and wrapped her arms about herself. The reality of what Kallie said sunk in, and she knew now how much not only she, but Merick too, risked bringing her to safety. Some had already given their lives. Melanie put her hands over her face. "Stop. Stop!" she begged, the truth of Kallie's words penetrating her hopes.

"Besides, in order to gain my lord's trust, you must surely give yourself to him."

"I had not thought about that," Melanie said, her face looking horrified.

"Although escape is not an option, I think perhaps there might be a way to gain your freedom." Melanie looked hopefully at Kallie, and when Kallie saw she had her full attention, she continued. "Though my lord is stubborn and arrogant, he is not a cruel man."

"Really?" Melanie said doubtfully, remembering Desmond lying motionless on the ground after Dragon had ruthlessly dispatched him.

"If he were cruel, he would not grant you the time you need to recover from your illness. He would have forced himself on you the moment you arrived and gone ahead with the wedding post haste."

"True," Melanie allowed.

"But if you suddenly became very unappealing to him, and he decided he did not want you for his bride, he would not just caste you from his gates to await your fate."

"He would not?"

"Nay, he would return you to your home, unscathed. I am certain of it," Kallie assured her. "At worse, you could expect him to ransom you."

"But how would I disenchant him? My father's money must tempt him sorely to risk so much."

"You must make yourself unappealing. He would not want you no matter how rich you stand to make him if he could not tolerate your presence."

"Are you certain?" Melanie asked, daring to hope what Kallie said was true.

"I am certain."

"But how do I go about making myself unappealing to him?"

Kallie smiled wickedly. "I think I have an idea."

~*~

"You want me to what?" Merick asked, certain he misunderstood de Brock's offer.

"I said I want you to train to be one of my men," Jamie repeated.

"I am only a player, my lord!"

Jamie leaned on the fence to watch the men practice

with their swords. Holden stood with his feet braced apart and gestured for a man to come at him. The clash of swords rang out, sending a shiver up Merick's spine. Surely de Brock did not mean for him to engage in the mock battles like the ones going on before him? These men, Dragon's soldiers, had been trained to fight since a tender age. Merick, too, could have taken up the sword as his brother Desmond had done, but he had never felt an interest in combat. He much preferred gentler pastimes, and only upon the insistence of his father had he leaned to fire a bow.

"Not all of my men have come from noble backgrounds. In fact, most of them are base born and have proven their merit by deed, some even earning their knighthood, as you may also."

Merick was shocked by de Brock's words. He had come into the dragon's lair to take back that which had been taken from him, by any means necessary, even vowing to challenge Dragon himself if it came down to it. And now, his enemy was offering to train him as one of his own men. The irony of it made him speechless.

"You have already proven your skill. I could use a man such as you."

The bait de Brock dangled before Merick's hungry eyes was far too tempting to be brushed aside. Far be it from him to turn down such a golden opportunity. Merick nodded his head before he thought too long on the offer, not allowing his doubts to outweigh his decision.

"I accept," he said to Dragon, then let his eyes stray to the tower in which his beloved Melanie remained. *Soon, my love*, he silently promised.

Chapter 10

Jamie looked up from his trencher when the doors to the great hall suddenly burst open. Expecting to see Lady Melanie coming to join him as he had ordered, he was disgruntled to see Kallie stride forward purposefully. Concern crossed Jamie's face when he took in the shocked and fearful expression upon the young woman's face.

"My lord! 'Tis Lady Melanie!"

Jamie took to his feet at once, readying himself to bark out the necessary orders if the Lady had attempted to escape. "Where is she?" he demanded.

Kallie reached out her hands beseechingly toward him. "An accident, my lord," she began, which was enough to send Jamie running from the hall, followed by half his men, toward the stairway.

Kallie hurried to keep pace with her lord's swift steps. He took the stairs three at a time and didn't slow his pace until he reached the stairs at the base of the tower room where Melanie had been kept a prisoner. In his haste, he almost trampled on the girl, who lay sprawled out at the bottom of the steps.

"My lady!" Jamie gasped, bending to touch the girl at his feet. There was a bit of blood on her cheeks and upon her chin.

Melanie groaned loudly when Jamie attempted to pull her bent leg out from underneath her body. It seemed that anywhere he touched her brought about loud howls of protest. He finally rose to his feet in defeat.

"I don't know what to do." He looked at Kallie desperately. "Get back, all of you," he yelled at the crowd of men, only allowing Tristan and Holden to get closer.

"Let me," Kallie said. She knelt down beside Melanie and gently straightened out her limbs the best she could. After slowly moving her neck and then her arms and legs, Kallie conveyed she did not believe anything to be broken. "She appears to be mostly bruised, my lord."

"But the blood...," he said.

Kallie carefully opened Melanie's mouth to check inside and jumped back slightly when she saw a big black gap where her two front teeth should have been. "Oh my," she whispered, leaning back so Jamie and the others could also see.

Melanie slowly reached up, putting her hand to her mouth, then groaned even louder, no doubt this time with despair over her disfigurement.

"How did this happen!" Jamie demanded, Kallie, receiving the brunt of his anger.

"I...I...was taking her to the hall as you requested, my lord," Kallie stammered.

"I did not tell you to throw her down the stairs!"

"She...she slipped. You cannot think, my lord, that I would do such a thing!"

Melanie, seeing her friend being attacked, began to

struggle to sit up. "My fault," she said.

"What?" asked Jamie, unable to make out the mumbled words Melanie attempted to speak.

"It is my fault. I lost my footing."

"'Tis hard to hear when you speak with your hand over your mouth, my lady," Holden told her.

Jamie glared at him and then turned his attention back to Melanie. "You slipped, you say? You were not pushed?"

Instead of speaking, Melanie instead gave an emphatic shake of her head.

Abashed, Jamie looked at Kallie. "Well, that's settled then," he said in way of an apology. "Should I take her to the physician?"

Kallie gave him a nasty look before she instructed him to take Melanie back up to her tower room. "There are no empty beds left in the infirmary."

After Melanie was once again ensconced in her room, Jamie, Tristan, and Holden returned to the hall to continue with their meal.

"That went over quite well, I think," Melanie said, sitting up in her bed.

"For *you*, it did. Everyone thinks I tried to kill you," Kallie said indignantly.

"No, not now they don't. I relayed to them it was my own fault."

"I guess," Kallie pouted, then smiled broadly. "You groaned wonderfully! I vow they would never suspect we pulled the wool over their eyes!"

"Yes, what a success your plan was. And how clever of you to come up with the idea to have my teeth knocked out. What is this black stuff, by the way?" Melanie asked, pulling at the sticky concoction that covered her front teeth.

"Tree sap, mixed with ash to darken it."

"Ingenious! And the bit of blood on my face was just the right touch to make it appear more believable. It hardly hurt my finger at all."

"It will be worth it, you will see. With the damaged leg I will declare you have sustained, Lord de Brock will not demand your presence in the hall for meals for a while yet. And with no teeth, I must admit I find you quite unattractive!"

"Let us just hope your lord does also," Melanie said. "But even if my leg was injured in the fall, I cannot expect that he will let me keep away from the hall for over long."

"Do not fret, for I have another plan for when that time arises," Kallie assured her.

~*~

Merick was late entering the great hall to take his supper, as he had returned to his quarters to wash and change his clothing. After agreeing to train as one of Dragon's men, de Brock had wasted no time in outfitting Merick in more appropriate attire. He'd given him a pair of shirts and breeches to train in and to wear about the castle, for Merick had only the player's outfit he had arrived in. As Merick took his seat and began reaching for some bread, one of the fellows across from him smiled broadly.

"Too bad you missed all of the excitement," he said.

Puzzled over the man's meaning, Merick looked at him. "Excitement?"

"Aye. It seems the lord's pretty little hostage threw herself down the tower stairs, no doubt to escape the wedding."

Merick almost choked on the piece of beef he'd put in his mouth. This was Melanie the man was speaking of, his beloved. Trying to mask his overwrought emotions, Merick started to question him, making his voice sound nonchalant. "De Brock holds a hostage?"

"Aye, in the tower. He brought her back with him from a tournament to be his bride," the man said.

"Though not willingly!" another man revealed, making the others chuckle.

"Why must he force a woman to be his bride? Surely with his reputation, he could find someone willing."

"His reputation has scared most women away," answered the man.

"Aye, and Tenebrous is not what most ladies would consider a good place to make a home," added another man at the table.

"But de Brock is the king's champion. He is renowned for his skills in battle. His riches alone should be enough to attract a bride," Merick argued.

"He may be the king's champion, but fat lot of good that does him. Edward gave him Tenebrous for his loyalty, but not the coin to keep it up."

"He has need of coin?" Merick asked.

"Aye, very much. 'Tis why he stole a wealthy lady. Lord de Brock cannot take the time to bother wooing a lady and asking for her hand the regular way — time is of the essence."

"Oh," Merick said, feeling a sense of relief wash over him. De Brock had not taken Melanie because he was smitten by her beauty, as Merick had feared. Taking her back if the man fancied himself in love would be a difficult task indeed. But if de Brock only lusted after the coin Melanie could bring him, he may be able to talk him into ransoming her instead. Perhaps when they met up again in training, Merick would casually mention to de Brock that he'd heard talk of a lady in the tower. De Brock could take it from there. If he wished a confidant, then Merick could make the ransom suggestion. He stood a good chance of convincing him, considering the way the men around the table were talking. The last thing de Brock wanted or needed was an unwilling bride on his hands.

~*~

"If my leg is hurt, there is no fear of my escaping," Melanie said to Kallie after the young maid arrived to take away her supper tray.

"Aye, there is not," Kallie agreed, looking speculatively at the lady and wondering what she was up to.

"Then perhaps my door does not need to be locked," Melanie said, crossing her fingers Kallie would not question her.

"I told you, my lady, if you attempt to escape, you will face many more trials beyond the walls than you would face at Tenebrous."

"I only wish to wander a bit. Surely there can be no harm in that?" Melanie insisted.

"Only both our necks!" Kallie assured her. "I put a lot at stake staging that little accident with you. If Lord de Brock discovers we have deceived him, he will beat us both!"

Melanie wanted desperately to confide in Kallie. The maid had proven herself to be her ally, but she was still wary of her loyalty. It seemed, however, the only way she would be able to communicate with Merick would be with Kallie's help. Melanie took a deep breath and sent up a silent prayer she was doing the right thing.

"I must tell you something." Melanie patted the side of her bed, and Kallie placed the tray on the table and joined her. "That man, the player, he is not who he seems to be," Melanie said in a rush.

"Who is he then?"

"My betrothed. He has come to rescue me." Melanie watched for any signs of betrayal on Kallie's face. She risked much revealing her tale, and she hoped she was doing the right thing.

"You have only seen him from afar. How can you know for certain it is he?"

"This morning, he walked around the tower, and I saw him look up at my window. I know it is he, for I saw him clearly then. I tore a piece of my gown and dropped it down to him, so he knew I was here. He tucked the piece in his vest, hiding it away."

"His risk is great. He must love you very much."

"I know," Melanie said, feeling badly for all the unkind thoughts she'd had about Merick in the past. Always believing him to be a coward, and now he was doing the most heroic thing she had ever seen.

"What is his plan? He cannot mean to snatch you right out from underneath my lord's very nose."

"I do not know. We have not talked, and this is why I must see him — now, tonight. I must tell him of the danger he is in. I must tell him not to risk his life for me."

"Surely, he must be aware of the danger he faces. Do you really think after doing so much, he will simply walk away just because you tell him to?"

"Aye, he will do as I ask. He always has. Only I must convince him I do not need his help. I will tell him you and I have already begun to clear a path to my release."

Kallie didn't look convinced. "I don't know if I should do this, but I will bring him here to you tonight. Then you can tell him he must leave Tenebrous, for his life is in danger."

"If you bring him to me, I will convince him, and he will leave. He must," Melanie said determinedly.

"Then I shall. At midnight," Kallie said, before taking the tray and leaving Melanie alone to pray the maid was not going to betray her, dooming her and Merick both.

~*~

"My love! I cannot believe my eyes!" Melanie cried.

"Shhh!" Kallie hissed urgently. "I had to toss my candle over the balcony to distract the guard on the second floor."

Melanie had jumped to her feet the moment she heard her door push open, and her eyes were greeted with a most welcome sight. Merick stood in the doorway, uncertain and slightly weary, wondering where the mysterious maid had led him this late at night.

And then he saw Melanie.

So many emotions flooded him all at once—relief, love, hope, and then regret. For if it had not been for his cruel words at the tournament, perhaps none of this would have happened. Was it only eight days ago? It felt like a lifetime since he had last seen her.

Kallie watched anxiously as the couple embraced. "I can only give you a moment together. My lady, you know what needs to be said," she reminded Melanie as she slipped out the door and closed it gently behind her.

Merick stepped back slightly but continued to hold Melanie's arms after hearing Kallie's words. "What does she mean, 'what needs to be said'?" he asked.

Melanie dropped her tearful gaze from Merick's eyes to his chest. He wore a shirt and breeches but the ties of both hung loose, displaying the fact he had quickly dressed. His hair was tousled, hanging wildly to his shoulders, and his face still showed the vestiges of sleep. His scent was familiar, and Melanie breathed deeply, desperately taking each moment with him at its fullest while he was with her. It may be a long, long while, she knew, before she may see his dear face again.

"You are in grave danger, my love," Melanie began gently, knowing her words may hurt Merick's fragile pride.

"We are both in danger," Merick corrected her. "Tell me, Melanie, has he hurt you?"

Melanie's gaze was steady as she answered, her face now masking her fear and anxiousness. She knew her every word and action would be measured, and she must convince Merick to leave her, that she could handle this. "No, I have not been hurt. In fact, I have been treated very well."

Anger crossed Merick's brow. "Is that why you threw yourself down the stairs? Is that why he keeps you a prisoner in this tower?"

Melanie splayed out her hands and turned in a circle, displaying herself to Merick. "Do I look hurt to you?"

"No," Merick admitted, eyeing her critically. "Actually, you look more beautiful than ever. But I do not understand. The way the men spoke in the hall at supper made it sound like you were close to death."

"There, you see, our plan is working."

"Our plan?"

"Yes, Kallie's and mine. Kallie, the maid who brought you to me, she came up with most of the ideas, but I helped a little. She really is quite clever."

"What are you playing at, Melanie?"

Melanie didn't like the warning look in Merick's eyes. She did not want to be scolded like a child, not when she had come so far. "Kallie and I have devised a plan to get de Brock to return me home, or at least to ransom me instead of insisting on marriage."

"What plan?"

"Well, I at first pretended to be ill, so he would not insist I join him for meals. Plus, it kept him from expecting anything from me," Melanie added, embarrassed by her meaning, but she could see from Merick's frown he knew what she meant. "Then, Kallie and I staged this little accident of mine. She let de Brock know my leg was badly hurt, and...." She turned toward the table for a moment, and when she turned back, smiled widely at him.

"Dear Lord!" Merick gasped, staring horrified at Melanie's gaping smile. "What happened to your teeth?"

Melanie took a moment to pull the sticky concoction from her front teeth. "Kallie made it. Is it not genius?"

Merick looked at the sticky mound Melanie held in her hand. "That was quite shocking, Melanie, I must admit."

"And it makes me most undesirable, does it not, my love?"

"Aye."

Melanie put the sap on the table and went to clasp Merick's hands. She looked up at him and smiled again. "You see, I have everything under control. You must leave Tenebrous, and before you know it, we will be together again."

"You want me to leave?" Merick said, not believing what she was asking of him. "After all I did to insinuate myself into the castle, you want me to simply walk away?"

The pain she saw cross Merick's brow made Melanie hesitate only slightly. If she had to hurt him in order to save him, she would do it. It had become instinctive to her over the years to protect Merick from harm—she must do this for his own good. "I got myself into this mess. I can get out of it. But I need to know you are safe."

Merick backed away from her in shock. The look on her face told him all he needed to know. Melanie was again protecting him, as she always had. She did not trust him enough to save her. But then again, when had he ever done anything but get her into danger? Though she claimed this latest disaster was her own doing, he knew it was his words that had driven her off to be alone, thus making her accessible to be captured. And now she wanted him gone, so she could again save herself because she knew he could not. He was only in the way.

Kallie pushed open the door and regarded the pair. "You must return to your room," she told Merick.

Melanie quickly rushed to throw her arms tightly around him. She kissed him, trying to ease the pain she knew she had caused. "I do love you so much, my darling. Please do not doubt this. But you must leave Tenebrous. I will be fine."

Merick clasped Melanie's slight form to him and rested his chin briefly on her head. "I love you, Melanie. And though I do not deserve it, I want you to trust me. This time, I swear it upon my very life, I will save you," Merick said, then turned to hurry from the room before Melanie could say any more.

Chapter 11

The laughter from the great hall rang in Melanie's ears as she climbed the stairs toward her tower room. Even from two floors away, she could still hear the howls that had erupted as soon as the doors closed behind her. She would have loved to run up the stairs, so great was her embarrassment, but the sham of being nearly lame made her trek slowly and ungainly. It didn't help that Kallie—no doubt to remind her of her portrayed predicament—had wrapped layers of cloth tightly around her limb. And truthfully, Melanie admitted to herself, as she pushed her tower door open wide and stepped within, she just might have forgotten the ruse without the reminder. But after spending only minutes in the hall, the bandages felt like they were cutting off her circulation.

Melanie secured the door and hiked up her skirts. Just as she went to sit down on the bed to unwrap her leg, a knock sounded. She dropped her skirts before opening the door. Seeing it was only Kallie, she went back to her bed and began unwrapping herself.

Kallie closed the door and leaned against it with a satisfied sigh. "That was brilliant!"

Melanie smiled up at her friend. "Thank you."

Kallie couldn't help but wince when she saw Melanie's lack tooth grin. "My word, you look a sight,"

"Well, I look better than I smell." Melanie made a face at the bandages piling up on the floor. "Whatever you soaked these with sure does stink."

"I had hoped the smell would not be quite so potent once they dried, but I fear I was wrong."

Melanie stood and picked up the rags, dumping them across the room beneath an open window. "Let us hope they air out a bit overnight." She sat down at the table and picked up a piece of leftover bread from that morning's breakfast.

Kallie walked over and sat down in the other chair. "Sorry, I didn't think to bring you up a tray. You did not get to eat very much below."

Melanie shrugged her shoulders while she swallowed down the hard bread with some warm ale. "It might have looked suspicious if you had since I told Lord de Brock I was feeling nauseous from the smell."

"That was not exactly a lie, I suspect," Kallie giggled.

Melanie grinned at her. "Not exactly."

It had been a week since she'd faked her fall from the tower steps. Kallie had put off her lord as long as she could, but when he'd insisted upon Melanie's presence during supper, Kallie could no longer deny him. They did not, however, have to make it an enjoyable interaction.

Melanie had appeared in the hall for the meal, but she had purposely arrived late. Dragon had already been seated, as had most of the men. She had hobbled across the hall toward him, each step making him more and more uncomfortable at the obvious distress he was causing her. Melanie's face had reflected her agony, not purely an act, for she had been truly terrified.

After she had stumbled — on purpose — three of de Brock's men had rushed over to assist her. Once they'd been close enough to catch wind of her, however, they had slowed their pace. One man had backed away entirely, so put off by her pungent odor, but the other two had bravely taken her arms. Melanie, holding her walking stick tightly in her grip, had smiled gratefully up at the pair, dazzling them with her toothless grin. The men had looked at her in horror before masking their expressions. Arriving at the lord's table, they'd deposited her by her chair at Dragon's right before hurrying off to their own seats.

De Brock had tried to hide his revulsion to the smell coming from the lady he'd said was to become his bride, but Melanie could see how much it bothered him. He kept trying to hold his breath, but when she'd attempted to make small talk, he had been forced to speak. She'd noticed how he tried to breathe only through his mouth. And then he had seen her smile. Though he had been prepared for her lack of teeth, he had stared at her face like she was something awful he had stepped in. He ate slowly, hesitant to take food from the trencher they shared.

After Melanie could no longer stand the pain in her leg, she'd been forced to resort to more sabotage. She made her hands shake whenever she reached over de Brock's lap for a morsel. Melanie knew he could see the trembles, for he watched her fingers warily every time she picked up bits of meat with sauce. She deliberately dripped sauce in his lap every time she reached over him. Crumbs from the dry bread were next. And then she'd gone for the cup of ale. The front of her gown was damp with her earlier attempts to drink, and in truth, it had been quite a task considering she'd not wanted to loosen the blackened sap on her teeth. But this time, she dropped the cup and its contents in de Brock's lap.

"God's teeth!" he'd exclaimed, jumping to his feet. And in that moment, Melanie feared she had gone too far. But Dragon was not the only one who was standing. Melanie had looked across the hall while Dragon attempted to sop up the front of his breeches, and her gaze had landed on Merick.

Their eyes had met and locked, and Melanie could see Merick had been about to spring forward in her defense if she should require aid. She'd stared at him, first in fear that he would do something rash and give them both away, and then in anger. He had ignored her pleas to leave this place and to let her get herself out of danger. Indeed, as she watched him retake his seat, she noticed how different he looked in only one short week.

It might have been a trick of the light, but Merick seemed somehow bigger. Not taller, but broader and more muscular. His face, usually clean-shaven, had a shadow of dark stubble that made him appear more masculine, and Melanie admitted to herself, quite appealing. The clothes he wore were the simple, everyday shirt and breeches he had worn that night to her tower room, but they seemed smaller on him, too tight across his arms and chest. Melanie had turned her attention back to de Brock, who was regarding her like she was a naughty child.

"I think it might be best for you to return to the tower," he'd said to her. Dismissed, Melanie had made her own way from the hall, unassisted.

"Merick is still here," Melanie informed Kallie. She'd risen from her seat and gone to stand under the window that didn't have the smelly rags beneath it. The small room had begun to stink, and Melanie was tempted to take the rags and throw them out the window.

Kallie frowned at her. "I know the smell is bad, but it is necessary if you wish to keep my lord from getting near you. I will ask him tomorrow when he is in a better mood if you can be allowed the freedom to roam the castle," she said, ignoring Melanie's comment about Merick.

"Do you think he will allow it?" Melanie asked hopefully.

Kallie put a finger beneath her chin as she pondered the possibility. "He knows there is no danger of you attempting to flee. And I will tell him if there is ever a chance of you walking without a limp, you need more exercise than this tower allows."

"Good, then I can find Merick and demand that he leave this place."

"You tried that already—he does not seem willing to obey."

Melanie began to pace in frustration. "What does he think his presence will accomplish? He cannot very well just grab me and steal me right out from under Dragon's nose."

"I think you should leave him alone. He does not appear to be in any danger. If my lord decides he will release you, or ransom you, then Merick can find his own way out of Tenebrous."

"You truly believe he is not in any danger?" Melanie looked at Kallie hopefully.

"Nay, believe it or not, my lord seems quite taken with him. I heard he even went out on the field himself to engage him in a training battle."

Melanie cringed. She could envision the look of fear she knew so well on Merick's face whenever he faced a fight. And she or Desmond would not have been there to help him. How frightened he must have been to face Dragon by himself!

"He held his own, I heard."

"What?" Melanie said, breaking from her trance.

Seeing the strain of worry etched across her brow, Kallie went over and put a comforting hand on Melanie's shoulder. "I said, he held his own."

"He did?" Melanie's voice was no more than a whisper as she contemplated Kallie's words. Was this the same Merick she was talking about? The man who had to be saved practically thrice a week?

"Aye. Tristan said he has run him ragged from dawn 'til dusk every day."

Melanie moved around Kallie and went to sit on the bed. She recalled seeing Merick in the hall tonight and had noticed the definite changes in him. Not only did he appear broader, but he had a confidence about him. He had stood up when he thought she was in danger and appeared ready to fight, and all without a moment's hesitation.

"I saw him in the hall tonight. I noticed how different he seemed," Melanie confessed.

"Well, you're not the only one who has noticed."

Melanie was not certain she liked the tone of Kallie's voice. "What do you mean?"

"It is that other player, Bevenly, I believe her name is. She has recovered from her injuries and has dogged Merick's every move, I have heard."

Melanie contained a growl she felt erupting from her throat. She suddenly wanted to tear the hair from Bevenly's head and chase her away from Merick. This feeling was something new to her, and it confused her greatly. Was she jealous? Never before had she experienced such unexpected resentment and anger and against someone she didn't even know. Merick was so innocent and kind, he would not see Bevenly's behavior for what it truly was—a blatant attempt to steal him away from Melanie. He would think the woman was just being friendly. She must protect Merick from Bevenly and her wickedly deceptive wiles. But first, she must get out of this room.

~*~

Merick was just about to enter his room when he heard footsteps behind him. He thought it might be the guard making his rounds but then realized the tread was much too light. He turned and saw Bevenly approaching him, appearing to be out of breath.

"My lord…I mean, Reginald," she said, hurrying to correct her slip.

Merick looked at the young woman with concern. Her pretty face seemed pinched with worry, and he feared they may have been found out. "What is it, Bevenly?" he asked.

Seeing she had Merick's full attention, Bevenly took advantage of the moment and drew out her response. She turned away from him and lowered her face into her hands as though she was much distressed. Her display achieved the desired effect. Merick put his arms around her shoulders in comfort and turned her gently back to him. When he pulled her in close to his chest, Bevenly tilted up her head, so her lips were angled toward Merick's face.

"I have been so frightened. Lord de Brock, he watches me, and I fear he suspects I am guilty of something."

"You have nothing to feel guilty about, Bevenly. You do not pretend to be something you are not. You are a player, and how you came to be in Tenebrous was not under false pretense."

"But you are not what you pretend to be. You are not only a simple player. And because I know this, I am as guilty as you."

Bevenly's words had been but a whisper, but Merick

feared her meaning all the same. He opened the door of his room and stepped inside, pulling her with him. What they spoke of must be in utmost discretion and not overheard.

Once in his room, Bevenly seemed to visibly relax. When Merick closed the door and locked it, he turned around and almost ran right into her. She looked up at him, desire in her eyes. She did not move away but instead reached her arms up behind his head and thrust her bosom into his chest.

Merick licked his lips, which had suddenly gone dry. The gown Bevenly wore was not her usual player's garb, and he figured she had been given clothing just as he and Melanie were. Her hair hung loose and just brushed her hips in long dark waves. She was slim but lusciously curved. Merick remembered how she had extended an invitation to him on their journey here to join him in her bed. Though she had not exactly said those words, her meaning had been clear. And now, her eyes held the same gleam in them.

"I hold a great secret in my hands," she whispered.

"Aye, you do."

Before Merick had a chance to react, Bevenly pressed her lips firmly against his. She clung to him, pushing her lower half wantonly against his hips. Merick took but a moment to get over his shock. He pried her hands loose, which were holding his shoulders in a desperate grip, and gently set her from him.

Bevenly looked up at Merick in confusion, so certain he would welcome her tonight. The expression on his face told her she had been mistaken. She walked over to stand before the window beside his bed. "I have made a great sacrifice in coming here. I have given up my only family, the players, and my livelihood. I have nothing. No home, no money, no friends — except for you, Merick," she said, daring to call him by his name.

"Things did not turn out the way they were supposed to," Merick reminded her. Though he felt badly for what had happened, he had finally come to realize he could not be held responsible. In the week since his arrival, Dragon's men had ridden out twice to chase off Fontleroy's men. The attacks this week had been more of an annoyance and not the deadly planned sabotage committed earlier. But the raids had enforced to Merick the fact that he had no control over what had happened. He and the players had just had the misfortune to arrive when they did. Although, thinking of the lives he had saved that day, Merick had to wonder if his timing had been destined.

"We did not enter Tenebrous the way we had planned, but you still have the chance to rescue your lady, and then you will leave this place. What will happen to me then?"

Merick hadn't really thought about what he would do with Bevenly. The original plan had been to see the players leave the castle and he be left behind. But that plan had obviously changed. Perhaps he could take Bevenly with him? Though he must admit, it would be difficult to escape with two women in tow. Leaving Bevenly behind would be his best chance at escaping with Melanie, but he wasn't sure he liked the thought of leaving Bevenly to her fate.

"I will come up with a plan," Merick assured her. "Perhaps there is something you could do here? I have noticed there are not many women around. Surely de Brock could use another laundress or a server?"

"Or a whore?" Bevenly sneered at him.

Merick was shocked by the change in Bevenly's expression. She had looked at him so sweetly but a moment ago, and now she looked as though she wished to throttle him.

"I did not say that!"

Bevenly put her hands on her hips and stalked toward him. "You did not have to. I can see by the look in your eye, now that you are safely in Tenebrous, I am no further use to you. Even now, you are thinking of a way you can leave me behind when you escape with your precious lady."

"Nay, I only want what is best for you," Merick assured her.

"I will tell you what is best for *you*, my lord, and that is to see I do not decide to go to de Brock and tell him what is going on!"

"Surely you would not, for your life too would be in danger then."

Bevenly smacked her hands against her thighs in frustration. "My life is already in danger, and it will be even more so if you leave me behind!"

"Then you will come with us," Merick said. He wasn't sure how he would pull it off, but it seemed Bevenly wasn't giving him much choice in the matter.

"You will take me with you?" Bevenly asked, not convinced by Merick's assurance.

"Aye, I will."

"Promise me, Merick."

Merick looked at her with resignation. "I promise."

Bevenly smiled then. She stepped around Merick and put her hand on the door. "There is one other thing," she said.

"What is it?" Merick asked wearily.

"Some of Dragon's men have made advances toward me. I did not wish it to continue, so I told them you and I are lovers."

Merick stood stunned as she continued.

"I expect you to play your part convincingly," she said, before she slipped from his room.

Chapter 12

The late August sun beat down upon the cobbled stones of the garden walkway, the quaint trail meandering through the tall rose bushes and beautiful wildflowers. The garden, which was surrounded by tall rows of hedges, was situated to the back of Tenebrous. Melanie had been delighted when she came across it quite unexpectedly on her first journey around the castle. She had poked around indoors all morning, walking the corridors of the five floors, but not brave enough to climb to the parapet and face the several guards above.

At first, she had been wary as she hobbled her way around the castle, fearful she would run into de Brock, and he would rescind her new freedom. But when she had spotted him from the solar window as she toured the third floor, she had relaxed. He had been training in the field below with his men, and Melanie had watched them for a time, hoping to catch a glimpse of Merick. She had not been disappointed.

Just as she was turning away, about to return to take the mid-day meal in her tower room, she had caught sight of him.

As he'd strode out across the field to meet his opponent, Melanie had been transfixed, and though she tried, she could not look away.

The first stipulation from her captor in his rules for her freedom were that Melanie take all meals in her tower room. She was not to enter the great hall unless bidden to do so. It being almost midday, Melanie knew Kallie would be soon arriving in the tower with her meal, but Melanie could not leave the window. Surely, she had reasoned, de Brock would not deny his men sustenance, and they would soon quit the field. So she had remained.

The battle had not lasted long. The other men, after finishing their matches, leaned against the fence to watch Merick spar with Holden. The two were evenly matched in size and weight, and after seeing Merick was holding his own, Melanie began to relax. He wielded his sword like an expert, slashing and blocking Holden's blows like he'd been training as a warrior for years and not just days. By the time the match was over — called by de Brock, who'd growled that the men would be there all day — the pair had been exhausted. Sweat had glistened all over Merick's chest, which he'd bared once he put down his sword. Holden, too, had removed his shirt, but Melanie had eyes only for her betrothed.

Now, as she stood alone in the garden, she recalled how Merick had walked off, out of her sight, with the other men. She'd remained at the window for a moment, mostly to steady her breathing, which had suddenly become labored and unsteady. Surely, she'd assured herself, it was all the walking she'd done that made her feel so flushed and anxious. It couldn't be the sight of Merick. But now, she was not so sure.

Who was this man who had once been her sweet and

gentle Merick? The man she'd seen at the hall last eve and the one on the field today was not the man she remembered. Merick would not have walked out fearlessly to meet a knight in battle with swords, even if 'twas just for practice. Her Merick may have jumped to his feet, ready to come to her aid as he'd done last night at supper, but he would not have looked so confident and unafraid. Nay, this was not her Merick. He had changed.

"Melanie?"

The voice which called to her was soft, and Melanie barely heard it until she heard the sound again. She turned slowly, suddenly uncertain if she was some place she should not be. But the gentle voice had not come from someone wishing to scold her. It had come from Merick, who now stood less than ten feet away from her. Her first instinct had been to rush toward him and throw herself into his arms. But as she'd stepped forward, she almost tripped over her crutch and was reminded of the part she must play.

Merick saw her uncertainty, and after a quick look around to make sure no one was watching, he started forward. He stopped when he stood close enough to reach out his hand to touch her. But he did not. Encouraged by the look of longing he'd seen on her face, Merick was hopeful she would not be angry with him. The last time they had been together, she had told him to leave Tenebrous and to let her find her own way out of this mess. He had not listened, but instead, he'd trained even harder with Dragon's men, resolved that he would save Melanie despite her objections.

Last night in the hall, it had been so difficult for him to watch her stumble across the floor to de Brock. Though he'd known it was only an act, he had still felt badly for her. Adding to her fear was also the humiliation she'd endured when the men had reacted to her gaping smile. Merick had also noticed the men seemed revolted by her, and after they'd deposited her beside de Brock, he'd displayed the same scrunched up look on his face. It was as though he was inhaling something very foul. Merick, now inhaling the scent himself, realized the girls had done something else to make Melanie even more unappealing.

Melanie fought the urge to reach out to Merick. It was true he had disobeyed her wishes and remained at Tenebrous despite her fear for his safety. But part of her was glad he'd remained. Knowing he was close by alleviated some of her loneliness. Kallie was becoming a dear and trusted friend, but she could not replace the bond Melanie had with Merick. She craved his touch, and felt overcome with longing to be embraced in his strong arms once again.

"How are you?" Merick asked, keeping his hands tightly against his sides.

Melanie smiled though her eyes were becoming moist. "I am well."

Merick noticed the gape in her smile and resisted the urge to stare at it. The smell of her was permeating the air around him, and he took an involuntary step backward. "I fear to linger lest we be discovered," he explained when he saw the pained look on her face.

When it looked like he was going to turn and leave, Melanie couldn't help but leap forward and latch onto his arm. "Wait!" she cried softly before releasing him.

"I dare not, my love," he whispered. Merick turned away, but when he heard Melanie choke back a sob, he stopped.

"Do not leave me," she begged.

Her voice was so pitiful, Merick couldn't help but turn back. "If we are discovered, all will be lost," he reminded her.

"I do not care!"

Merick looked quickly around the garden, hopeful no one had heard her outburst. "Shhh!" he warned her.

"I am so tired of this! I want to go home."

"So do I."

Melanie reached up to pull the sticky sap off her teeth and held it in her hand. Trying to talk when it was on was difficult, and she didn't like the way Merick kept staring at her mouth. The smell from her leg was giving her a headache—even the sweet scents from the garden failed to cover it up. It was no wonder Merick seemed anxious to escape her presence.

"How are things going with de Brock? You do not think he suspects who you truly are?"

"Nay, he treats me no differently from the other men."

Melanie knew from Kallie that Merick had been regarded as somewhat of a hero around Tenebrous since his encounter with Fontleroy's soldiers. Too, Dragon himself had asked Merick to stay on and train to be one of his men. This should have reassured her Merick was safe, but for how long? And what about the player Bevenly that Kallie had said was following Merick around like a lovesick girl? That woman knew who Merick truly was. What if she accidentally messed things up for them?

"I have heard that the woman, the player who was brought in a week ago, has recovered." Melanie tried to make her voice sound casual.

Merick had a flash of last night rush back to him. He had seen Bevenly watching him this morning as he trained, her eyes burning into him. He knew he was supposed to play the part of her lover—if he didn't, her threat to expose him had been clear. But now that Melanie was allowed to roam the grounds as she liked, she was certain to see him and Bevenly together. It might be easier to explain his situation now, instead of having to grovel later.

"Melanie, I should tell you something, but I must warn you first. You are not going to like it."

"What is it, Merick?"

"The player, Bevenly is her name. She is worried what is to become of her once you and I make our escape."

Melanie hadn't been partial to the plan, so she did not know how things were supposed to play out. "I take it your plans got changed when you and the others were caught up in the skirmish outside the gates. I know the other players were killed, and I was very sorry to hear that."

"Aye. Well, Bevenly and the others were to only stay on for a couple of days and then depart Tenebrous together, leaving me behind for some reason. Now that is no longer possible."

"I see," Melanie said.

"I did not expect things to turn out this way, and I must admit that last night when Bevenly confronted me, I did not know what to say to her."

"You are forgetting Kallie and I have a plan of our own. If it works, which it already seems to be doing, then de Brock will ransom me or even just set me free. Kallie assures me either way, he will provide me with safe passage home. After I am gone, you can tell de Brock you wish to leave—there is really no reason for him to make you stay on. And, since you and Bevenly are supposed to be friends anyhow, it would only seem natural for her to wish to leave with you."

Melanie made it all sound so simple, but Merick knew things didn't always turn out the way you wanted them to. "There is something else. Bevenly told me the men have been making advances toward her."

Melanie wasn't really surprised because she'd noticed there were hardly any women around Tenebrous at all. "I could ask Kallie to wrap some stinking bandages around her. I know it has kept the men far away from me."

"I am afraid she has already come up with a plan to keep the men away."

"What is it?" Melanie wasn't sure she wanted to hear this plan, judging by the look on Merick's face.

"She told them she and I are lovers."

Melanie gasped in outrage. "She cannot expect you to play the part!"

Merick sighed. "I fear I have no choice in the matter."

"Why ever not?"

"She threatened to expose me if I did not."

Melanie began to pace amongst the flowers, careful to exaggerate a limp in case anyone happened to look. She could not believe the nerve of that woman! Bevenly knew Merick was betrothed to someone else, and yet she wanted him to act like he was her lover! If Bevenly were here right now, she would have gladly pulled her hair out by the roots!

Merick knew that feral look on Melanie's face all too well. She got it right before she was about to attack someone. "Please, my love, do not get angry," he tried to soothe her.

Melanie stopped pacing and glared at Merick. "How can you expect me not to get angry? Let us see how much she can reveal to de Brock with all of her teeth knocked out!"

"It would look suspicious if you were to attack Bevenly in a jealous rage. You and I are not even supposed to know each other. Indeed, we risk much even talking here right now. What if someone were to come across us?"

Melanie knew Merick was right. She took deep breaths to

calm herself. "Make it clear to her you are only doing this to keep us all safe. Tell her I should be gone soon because de Brock is sickened by me. Any day now, he could be sending me home. Tell her you can leave together after it is safe." The thought of Merick traveling all the way back to Balan Castle with that harlot in tow made Melanie feel uneasy. The girl fancied herself in love with Merick, and now she could be spending several days and nights alone with him. Melanie knew if she could run off with Merick right now, she would, Bevenly be damned.

"I will make it clear to her it is only an act," he assured her.

"Good. Besides, if you only engage in a little hand holding, that should be more than enough to make the other men think you are a couple."

Merick wasn't so sure. The way Bevenly had thrown herself at him last night made him think she might be after more than just hand holding.

"What happened, by the way, at the tournament? Were my parents very worried about my safety?" Melanie asked, changing the subject.

"Aye, we were all worried."

Melanie saw the way Merick suddenly became interested with a thread on his tunic. He was avoiding looking at her, and she thought she knew why. He undoubtedly blamed himself for what had happened to her.

"Merick, I do not want you to feel responsible for de Brock taking me. It was my own foolishness that had me walking off alone in the forest."

He looked at her with regret. "Nay, you were there because you were angry about what I had said. I falsely accused you of having feelings for de Brock. Too, I even released you from our betrothal. I am ashamed to tell you that after you went missing, I just assumed you and he had run off together."

Melanie had thought as much. "It is over now, Merick. I do not blame you."

"You should. If Desmond had not convinced me you would never have run off like that, I might still be catering to my injured pride at home. 'Twas he who came up with the plan to rescue you. He would have come himself if he had not been hurt in the tournament."

"Yet, despite not knowing if I were truly in danger, you risked everything to come after me."

"After realizing you would not have left me willingly, I would have risked the fires of hell and fought the devil himself to save you, my love."

Melanie felt tears forming in her eyes again. It was so hard to keep her distance—she longed to touch him. "That is why you stayed when I asked you to leave."

Merick nodded.

"How is Desmond's leg?" she asked, wondering if Beatrice had stayed on at Balan Castle. She'd forgotten about how Beatrice had reacted when she knew Desmond was no longer an undefeated champion. She'd never had the chance to tell Merick how the woman had frightened her with her bizarre ranting.

"He was using a crutch when I left, but I am sure he will mend in time."

As much as Melanie wanted to tell Merick about Beatrice, she knew there would be time for that later after they were safely away from Tenebrous. Right now, they had more important matters to attend to.

Voices in the garden sounded, and Merick knew the time to leave had come. He gave Melanie one last look and then mouthed the words, "I love you."

Melanie watched him turn and stride quickly away. "I love you, too," she whispered.

Chapter 13

Melanie sat impatiently in her room, waiting for Kallie to arrive with her evening meal. She wasn't hungry for her supper. It was information she craved. When she heard the footsteps outside her door, Melanie rose from her bed and flung the door open wide.

"Finally!"

Kallie stepped inside and put the tray on the table. "I had no idea you were so anxious for the cook's veal."

Melanie looked at the food and scrunched up her face. The thing she missed the most besides her family and freedom was the meals from her own home. "I want you to tell me how you keep the men here from making advances toward you."

Kallie looked at Melanie. "How I keep the men from making advances?" She wasn't sure she'd heard her correctly.

"Aye, what do you do?"

"I am not quite sure I understand."

"Do you threaten them? Do you scream if they come near?"

"They do not bother me," Kallie said, anxious to end this conversation.

When Kallie looked like she was about to leave, Melanie blocked her path. "Beverly told Merick he must play the part of her lover in order to keep the other men away."

"Ahh." Now she understood. "So you want me to tell you what I do so Merick does not have to play along."

"Yes!"

Kallie walked over to sit down at the table and began nibbling on Melanie's supper. She was stalling on purpose. What she was about to reveal was going to shock the proper Lady Melanie. She could see her friend getting more anxious by the moment, and then when she seemed ready to explode, Kallie finally confessed her secret. "I belong to Dragon."

Melanie's mouth dropped open and remained that way for well over a minute. "You...."

Kallie sighed. "Yes, I do, and we have." She stood up and began to pace.

"But...." Melanie was at a loss for words. Whatever she had been expecting Kallie to reveal, this certainly had not been it.

"There is more."

Melanie sat down on her bed, suddenly very exhausted. "I am almost afraid to hear it."

"I have something to confess to you, and in telling you, you will hold my very life in your hands."

"As you hold mine and Merick's," Melanie reminded her.

"Yes, you have trusted me, and that is why I feel I can trust you." She paused only a moment, then blurted out, "I am not a maid. I am a lady, as you are."

Melanie had to stop her mouth from dropping open once again. "You are a lady?"

"I was traveling with my maid and several guards when we were attacked. My maid was killed, and while my men were engaged in a futile battle with the attackers, I quickly donned her clothing."

"Surely the men had seen you, though. They would not have been fooled by your disguise."

"Nay, probably not. But then the men who were attacking us were attacked. Another group of soldiers passing by saw what was happening. They slew the attackers and saved me. All my men were killed."

"What happened next?" Melanie asked, mesmerized by the tale.

"They did not have time to cater to a female and wished to dispose of me as quickly as possible, so they brought me here, to Tenebrous. They brought me as close to the gates as they dared and then fled."

"They did not seek a reward?"

"Nay, for I played the part of a maid. Revealing I was a lady may have made my circumstance more precarious."

"I take it you were allowed into the castle."

"Aye. Actually, my lord was very kind to me. I almost told him I was Lady Kallasanda Botenay — that is my name."

"So, why did you not?"

Kallie threw her arms up in the air in frustration. "I was afraid. I knew of Dragon's reputation. That he was looking for a wealthy bride, for we are practically neighbors. I hail from Kildran Castle, just north of Tenebrous."

This gave Melanie some hope. "If you live close-by, then perhaps you can escape with Merick and me. If we could get there, we could send a message to Balan Castle."

"But I do not wish to leave," Kallie said quietly. "Not

anymore."

Melanie was shocked that someone would actually choose to remain in the company of that overbearing beast.

"We became lovers after I had been here a fortnight."

"He forced you?" Melanie spat bitterly.

Kallie got a dreamy look in her eye. "Nay, I went to him willingly. His men had been bothering me, for there were no other women in Tenebrous—under the age of fifty, that is. But when my lord expressed an interest in me, his men, of course, backed off."

"I think I would have rather thrown myself from the tower."

Kallie smiled. "I would have thought the same thing. But he is different with me. He has always been gentle and kind."

"You are in love with him!"

"Aye."

Melanie stood and went over to her friend, putting her hands on her shoulders. "Then why do you not reveal yourself? He could marry you, and then he will let me go!"

Kallie turned away. "I cannot!"

Melanie didn't understand Kallie's hesitation. "If you love him and he cares for you, then what is the problem?"

"What do you think he will do when he finds out I have been lying to him all this time? Certainly, he might very well marry me if he can ever forgive me, but then he will have only done so for the wealth I can bring him. Would you want Merick if he did not want to marry you regardless of who you were?"

Melanie suddenly felt guilty, for she knew Merick would indeed want her even if she were a penniless maid. But she had not wanted him, really. She had constantly done battle with her conscience over whether she could really love him because he was not the type of man she wanted him to be. He had been weak and helpless. But now, he had changed. He was behaving like a warrior, brave and strong, and her desire to be with him had flared to life. Melanie was disgusted with herself. She was no better than Dragon.

"I can see by your expression that you would not," Kallie said.

Melanie didn't want to tell Kallie what she had been thinking. The realization that had occurred to her was something she wanted to ponder privately. She tucked her thoughts aside so she could concentrate on Kallie and her dilemma. "I want to help you as you have helped me."

Kallie smiled tightly. "I do not think there is anything that can be done about my situation. I cannot tell my lord who I am, yet I also cannot leave him."

"If our plan works and he ransoms me or even sends me home, then he will only steal himself another lady to wed. How long are you willing to endure this torture?"

Kallie turned away to look toward the window, suddenly wishing to escape this questioning. "I do not know."

"And if and when he does finally wed, do you think his bride will tolerate your presence?" Melanie could see Kallie's shoulders hunch even more, and she felt badly for her. But Kallie obviously hadn't thought things through. She owed it to her to wake her from the dream she had been living.

Kallie turned around to face her. "I secretly hope he will one day realize I mean more to him than coin. He is far from being a wealthy man, but I do not care. I love him for who he is, not for what he has. I only wish he could feel the same about me."

Melanie couldn't bear to see the pain in her friend's eyes. If it were up to her, she would march right up to that overgrown oaf and shake some sense into him. But that wasn't likely to happen.

~*~

Over the next three days, Merick continued to train with Dragon's men and even Dragon himself. It was easy to see why these men were so feared, considering the constant daily paces their lord put them through. De Brock never let them forget they were warriors first above all else.

They had acquired quite a following of spectators as they moved about the fields, training daily in swordplay, the quintain, and the joust. In his wildest dreams, Merick never would have thought he'd enjoy having people watch him. But as the days wore on, he became used to the castle folk who gathered when he and the men engaged in training.

A favorite of the people was the archery contests. Merick relished the adoration and was humbled by the roaring cheers as he outmatched every man in Tenebrous. The crowd had been especially loud, much to his delight and relief when he even bested the Lord of Tenebrous himself. Dragon had laughed good-naturedly, even slapping him on the back after Merick shot his last arrow — splitting Dragon's to pieces — claiming the bullseye for his own. When they matched swords, Merick — though growing stronger and more competent every day — fell each time from Dragon's ruthless onslaught. And as he'd lie on the ground, dazed and hurting, it reminded him of Desmond and the defeat he'd suffered at de Brock's hands. Merick sometimes felt overwhelmed by his rage and need for vengeance against this man — the man who had wreaked such havoc with his life. But then, later, as de Brock sat and drank with his men like he was one of them, and they laughed and joked together, Merick felt confused. The man he'd sworn to battle to the death, if need be, to free his dear Melanie was becoming his friend.

The hot afternoon sun scorched the men's bare chests, which dripped with perspiration as they wrestled in the dirt. Pillows of dust rose up to choke them if they forgot to hold their breaths. Merick pinned his opponent quickly with a heel to the throat, the way Tristan had shown him, then searched the crowd of cheering faces to seek out his lady.

He was not disappointed.

Melanie had hobbled over and stood by the fence watching him intently, her face a mask of worry. The relief she displayed when his opponent yielded was visible, and Merick couldn't help but feel slightly annoyed. Bevenly, too, watched at the fence. Merick could see her face showed not relief but shone with the unmistakable glow of desire. She had not looked like she was about to leap over the fence and throttle his opponent. Unlike his Lady Melanie, Bevenly had faith in him.

He strode to the gate and stepped outside, not hesitating to walk over to Bevenly. It had bothered him at first to continue to play this false game of love with the woman, but despite her earlier threats, Bevenly's company was quite enjoyable. As Merick approached, he saw she was holding a cool cloth for him. Instead of passing it into his waiting hands, she rubbed it eagerly over him, bathing his chest and muscular arms. He withstood her administrations with patience, knowing others were watching. He would swear he could feel Melanie's eyes burning a hole straight through his back, although, he thought, a little jealousy wasn't such a bad thing. Not when it made her seek him out every chance she got. Perhaps she might even soon realize he was no longer the milksop she remembered who needed constant rescuing.

Melanie's blood was boiling over. It was a good thing

the crowd had given her such leeway, or she might have lashed out at someone. As it was, no one would come within ten feet of her, for the smell from her leg was too terrible. The fools hadn't even realized she did not still wear the bandages, for she had taken them off in her room after lunch. The smell had given her a headache, and they were uncomfortably tight. Each day she'd been forced to cut short her outings so she could retire to her room to lie down. The bandages seemed to have done the job, though, for everyone at Tenebrous remembered the noxious scent and backed far away whenever she came near. But her lack of popularity was the least of her worries. Now all she could do was dig her fingernails into her crutch as she watched that harlot throw herself so shamelessly at Merick.

It didn't help Melanie's tattered confidence that she had to stumble around the castle smelling and gape-toothed like a fool. Especially damaging was Bevenly oozing sexuality, being so curvaceous and so blatantly available. Merick didn't seem to mind her attention despite his earlier grievances. Indeed, he seemed completely enraptured by the intimate care he received. Melanie could hear the suggestive comments aimed at the pair as Merick's new comrades passed by him. Comments about what he and Bevenly should do with the rest of the afternoon. She was especially shocked to hear him yell back that he just may take their advice.

Turning her gaze away from the pair, Melanie hobbled off slowly in the opposite direction. She suddenly felt nauseous, but this time she knew the cook's lunch was not to blame.

After a time, she became tired but did not yet wish to return to the confines of her tower room. What she needed was companionship. Kallie spent most evenings with her, chasing away the doldrums with her silly quips and laughter, making the best out of their situations. But Melanie was finding it harder and harder as the days stretched on to keep up her spirits. Everyone seemed to be moving forward and going on with daily life, but Melanie felt as though her life had been put on hold. Dragon had yet to inform her of what he planned to do with her. She didn't know if he still intended to wed her or if he had decided to ransom her. Kallie said he was still mulling his options over.

Melanie sat down on an upturned stump by a shed filled with firewood. Thankfully, no one was around to send her off, so she could rest a moment. She could see the castle inhabitants wandering the grounds, slowly returning to their work. It had become almost a daily habit now for them to group together, taking a break from their chores and duties, to watch the training of Dragon's men. Some of the fellows Merick trained with were squires, not yet ready for knighthood. But some of the older knights had taken part as well, mostly for the practice and exercise it gave them.

The sound of laughter caused her to turn and see a rowdy group of five young men approaching the direction of the woodshed. Melanie made ready to get up and move on before she was asked to leave. As she dragged herself to her feet, careful to make a slow task of it, she heard another sound. This sound, however, did not come from the approaching youths. It came from within the shed. Too loud to be a rat, she thought perhaps it was a dog. Melanie hobbled around to the other side of the shed, so she was out of sight of the group. After they walked past, she would open the doors and allow the animal out.

But the group did not walk past. They stopped before the shed, and Melanie could hear their voices.

"Are you sure he ran in here?" asked one of the fellows.

"Aye, it was either here or the barn," another answered.

Anger overtook Melanie, but she held her ground. They had obviously been teasing a poor animal, and it had taken refuge in the woodshed. She could practically hear its pathetic whimpering through the thin wall. Hopefully, with all the noise they were making, the bullies wouldn't hear it. Melanie held her breath, not releasing it until they moved on, deciding to search out the barn. After they disappeared into the larger building, Melanie hurried to pull open the door of the shed.

"Come on out, come on, you are safe now," she called softly, anxious to get the animal safely away.

She could hear movement at the back corner, and some of the stacks of wood rolled to the ground. Then slowly, a crouched figure began to advance. Melanie gasped in surprise as the figure stood upright and began to come closer. She backed away when she saw it was not an animal the young men had been after. It was a man.

Chapter 14

He was not exactly a man, not quite, but close to being one. He could not have been any older than Melanie was, but since she considered herself to be a grown woman, then he must be a man. He just looked so young, though. Even Merick, who was only a few years older than she was, seemed much older to her than this fellow. Perhaps it was the fearful look upon his face, the vulnerability that made him seem so young.

"They are gone," Melanie told him, trying to ease his tension.

"Thank you." His voice was no more than a whisper, and Melanie thought perhaps he was worried the bullies might be close. He did seem to relax slightly, though, and even managed a timid smile.

"I am Melanie. What is your name?"

He took a while to answer, and she wondered if he had not heard her.

"I am Samuel. Samuel Tolley," he finally replied.

It was obvious he'd been hiding in the shed from those

fellows. Melanie didn't want to make him more uncomfortable by asking why he had felt the need to conceal himself. He was afraid, plainly so, and embarrassed, no doubt, about his fear. She'd seen it many times in Merick, that fear, so she could understand his predicament completely. In fact, she suddenly felt more comfortable than she ever had since her arrival at Tenebrous. She was in her element, playing the role of protector and soothing damaged pride.

"It is completely unfair when a group thinks it a sport to gang up on one man. I vow, even Dragon himself would be hard pressed to take on all those fellows." Even as she said it, Melanie recalled that day at the pond when de Brock had brought low four miscreants without breaking a sweat. She pushed those thoughts aside, feeling suddenly anxious about remembering how infallible her captor was. Her goal was to make poor Samuel feel better, so making the observation was in his best interest, even if it wasn't true.

"Oh, nay! You are mistaken," he said, as though she had maligned a saint. "Dragon could take on a dozen men or more!"

Melanie didn't doubt it. She had made a poor comparison of de Brock and Samuel. "Any of the other men, then. They would surely find the odds unfair."

"Perhaps," he said, though he didn't sound convinced.

As much as Melanie was enjoying finding someone who didn't cringe at the sight of her, she was anxious to leave the shed. When those bullies failed to find their quarry in the barn, they may return here to search for him.

"Let us be off," she suggested.

Samuel needed no further urging, being just as eager as she was to be away.

As soon as they stepped out into the open, they heard the

voices. Melanie cursed her luck at having lingered too long. It was now too late to escape notice—the excited sounds coming from the group let them know they'd been spotted. Samuel froze. The mask of fear on his face told Melanie they were in a heap of trouble.

But, then again....

"Is that not the lady from the tower?" said one of the fellows, stopping short as the group ran up to halt the pair's escape.

The others stopped dead in their tracks at the mention of the tower lady. They were now close enough to see it, indeed, was she.

Melanie suddenly did not despise her reputation as a cesspit-smelling foul cat. All her days being branded an outcast had done her a great service. Not only did she keep de Brock at bay, but any other unwanted attention was also averted.

Like right now.

"Are you young men looking for me?" Melanie asked innocently, stepping forward to smile her gape-tooth grin at them.

The young men stepped back. "Ah, no, my lady, we were just seeking out our comrade, Samuel. We see you have found him and that he is well, so we will take our leave," one of them said.

"Are you certain you cannot linger with us a while?" She again stepped toward them, and they all took another step back.

"Nay!" They all declared in unison before making a wide arch around Melanie and running off.

Melanie laughed with glee, then turned to face Samuel. "I do not think they shall bother you any longer."

Samuel couldn't help but laugh. The sight of Melanie,

appearing so captivatingly beautiful — until she opened her mouth — was enough to make anyone chuckle. Or shock them speechless.

"Are you really she?" Samuel asked.

"Unless there is another lady hobbling around Tenebrous lacking her two front teeth and smelling like a garderobe."

~*~

"Kallie, you did not give me a chance to tell you about my new friend earlier," Melanie said when Kallie returned that evening to get her supper tray.

Kallie stepped inside the room but did not close the door all the way behind her. Melanie worried her friend would not stay, and she would have to spend the evening alone.

"I thought, perhaps, you would wish some company tonight," Kallie said, smiling coyly. She pushed the door wide and gestured to someone out in the hall.

"Merick!" Melanie gasped as her betrothed stepped forward.

He didn't waste any time taking her into his arms and giving her a passionate kiss. When he finally pulled away, it was to the sound of Kallie loudly clearing her throat.

"I guess I will be going now. I can come back in about an hour," Kallie told the pair, who still hadn't taken their eyes off each other.

"Make it two," Merick told her before he ushered her out the door and closed it securely.

"Merick! That was quite rude — you did not even give me a chance to thank her."

"Thank her after I am gone. We do not have much time."

As much as Melanie was glad to see him, she couldn't help but remember how he had acted in the yard. She had gone to watch him train with the others, and he had barely spared her a glance. But he'd had plenty of attention to give to Bevenly.

Merick frowned at the sour look he was suddenly getting. "Do not be angry, my love. You know I but played a part today with Bevenly."

Melanie covered her ears and turned away. "Do not speak her name in my presence!"

He turned her toward him and held her, stroking the length of her hair down her back. "Then let us speak of us. I will tell you of how I long for you. Even but a glimpse of your loveliness is a gift to ease the long day."

She blushed over his sweet words. This was the Merick she remembered, pretty words and gentle caresses. She knew deep down he did not care for Bevenly, but to see them together hurt her greatly.

"I heard you say to Kallie you made a new friend today," Merick said, distracting her from her thoughts.

"Aye," Melanie replied simply. She didn't want to talk about Samuel. He was a sweet fellow, but he had reminded her too much of her life with Merick outside of Tenebrous. As much as Melanie hated to admit it, she missed the way Merick had been. Before, his interest had been solely in her and family. Now he only seemed interested in combat and spending all his time with Dragon's men. She'd seen him at a distance, laughing and playing around with them. He'd seemed to be enjoying himself immensely with a bunch of men who were supposed to be the enemy.

Merick led her over to the bed where they could sit down comfortably and still hold each other. Melanie rested her head upon his chest, listening to the steady rhythm of his heartbeat. He lifted her chin and softy brushed his lips against hers. It didn't take long for him to get caught up in the contact, and his kiss became more urgent. His grip on her tightened, pulling her closer until Melanie's breasts were crushed against his chest.

When his tongue slipped into her mouth, Melanie was shocked, for he had never kissed her this way in the past. Before she could break away, he began to lean her back against the bed, his body resting gently upon her. Melanie's senses were reeling. She felt so hot, yet she did not wish for him to stop. It would not hurt, she assured herself, to enjoy the kiss. But then she felt his hand upon her breast. A new wave of heat surged through her. This time she felt it deep in her secret place. It confused her, this feeling. It was like she had suddenly lost control of herself. She wanted more, but of what she knew not.

Merick was overcome with arousal. He and Melanie had shared kisses before, but never something like this. Desmond had told him how he would get lost in madness when he kissed and fondled women, but Merick had never imagined it could feel this way. He was almost twenty and two, but he still had never been intimate with a woman. He had always known he would one day be with Melanie, and he had waited for her. They were betrothed — what would it matter if they were to seal their bond now instead of later? Too, the precariousness of their situation made Merick wonder if perhaps it might bode well for Melanie if she were not untouched. If Dragon tried to force their union, Melanie could prove she'd belonged to another. Dragon might not want her if she wasn't a virgin.

Melanie, try as she might to not do so, couldn't help but think about Dragon right now. The thought of him, doing to her what Merick was doing, sent a shiver of fear through her body. She trusted Merick completely and knew he would never do anything to harm her. That wasn't true of her unwanted host.

He would take her and think nothing of it, except for the coin he would gain in the end.

But then, Melanie remembered Kallie.

Kallie had said she and de Brock were lovers. That must be the reason why he had not forced her to be his. And now, he was so repulsed by her that surely he would not think of her in that way. She was safe, she was certain. Assured by her thoughts, she felt her longing for Merick intensify. She wanted him, and it was obvious he wanted her.

Merick mistook her tremor of fear for anticipation and forged ahead with his assault on her senses. By Melanie's quick intake of breath, he could tell she enjoyed what he was doing. His caresses became bolder. His hand found its way beneath her dress and began working its way up her calf. Melanie's legs were apart, and he nestled in between them, his manhood, hot and demanding, strained against the fabric of his breeches. He pushed himself against the juncture of her thighs, lifting himself up and swaying forward, making her moan in anticipation.

When Merick's hand touched her core, Melanie gasped. His fingers were gentle. She could feel them parting her nether lips and then seeking further inside. He held his body over hers as he explored with probing fingers. She writhed and twisted, grasping the bed sheets tightly in her fists.

Merick pulled Melanie's gown from off her shoulders and lowered it to bare her breasts to him. He suckled eagerly at her peaked buds while he undid the ties upon his breeches and freed his manhood, which soared free. He lifted her gown higher and centered himself between her legs.

"It shall only hurt for a moment, my love," he assured her as he poised himself before her opening.

Melanie readied herself as she felt him push inside, only

to be stopped by her maidenhead. She took a deep breath as she prepared for him to continue and then gasped as he surged onward. It was as he promised — the pain did not linger.

Merick waited patiently, holding himself still until he knew the discomfort had waned, and then he began to move inside of her. Long strokes, in and out, until Melanie was panting with pleasure. Then, faster and faster, he moved until he was on the brink of bursting. When he heard Melanie's cry of release, he could wait no longer to take his own pleasure. They were one. Together they soared, each of them caught up in the passionate throes of completion. Merick smiled and rested his forehead against Melanie's.

Finally, he understood what it was Desmond had been going on about.

Chapter 15

"I can tell by the look on your face something happened last night," Kallie said, eyeing her friend, who still sat in bed despite the late morning hour. Her legs were bent up under her chin, with her arms wrapped tightly around them.

Melanie tried to stop smiling. She finally gave up. "I am just so happy."

Kallie put the tray on the table and turned to face her. "You look like a woman who has been made love to."

Melanie blushed, unaware it could appear so obvious on her face. "How do you know?"

Kallie walked over to sit down beside her on the bed. "I was the same way."

"You were?" Melanie was relieved. She had begun to worry something might be wrong with her, and she might have to wear this silly grin on her face the rest of her life. It wouldn't have normally been a problem, but since she had to go about the castle with black sap over her teeth, it might become one.

"Don't worry. The effect will wear off soon," Kallie

promised.

"I hope not! I have never felt so glorious in all my life."

"Did it hurt?" Kallie asked her.

"Aye, a bit. Will it always be so?" Though the experience was mostly a pleasurable one, she had not liked the pain nor the blood.

"Nay. Next time there will be no pain, and you will not bleed again. 'Twas only the breaching of the maidenhead which made it so."

"Next time…." Melanie hadn't thought about that yet. But she supposed there would, of course, be more moments like the one she'd shared with Merick last night. The thought warmed her, and she felt a tingle of anticipation go through her body.

"Now that he has made you his, he will want you again and again," Kallie warned her.

The idea was not unpleasant to Melanie. "Again and again…," she said dreamily. "Was it so with you and your lord?"

Now it was Kallie's turn to blush. "Aye, it was."

"And will it be as enjoyable each time?" Melanie asked boldly.

"Each time has been wonderful," Kallie assured her.

"Wonderful…."

"Yes, it is. Now perhaps you should rise and dress. The sun is climbing, and it is promising to be a beautiful day."

Melanie rose from the bed and reached for a gown to wear. "Can you not spend some time walking with me this morn?"

Kallie sighed. "I wish I could, but I am needed in the sick room."

"Surely the men have recovered from the attack by now?" Melanie asked with concern.

"Most of them have, but there is still a fellow who had an

infection come on. He thrashes about with fever, but it should soon pass. The physician asked me to sit with him this morning while he tends to his medical supplies."

"I hope he is well soon."

"As do I. But then I must help Lilith serve the midday meal and then tidy up. And, of course, there is my lord's mending to attend to, and some washing to do—"

Melanie waved her hands in the air. "All right, all right! I know you are busy. I only asked because I'm so very lonely."

"Did I not hear you say last night you had made a new friend?"

"Oh yes, I did say that. I met a young fellow who was being chased by a bunch of bullies. His name is Samuel—he was hiding out in the woodshed."

"And he was actually brave enough to come close to you?" Kallie asked with surprise.

Melanie scowled. "I do not smell anymore!"

"I have noticed that. Let us just hope nobody else does."

Melanie gave her a worried look. "Do you still fear de Brock will try to force me to be his bride?"

Kallie looked thoughtful. "Nay, actually, I was just about to tell you I overhead him talking to Tristan last night. He said he was considering ransoming you."

"Did he!"

"Contain your excitement, for I also heard Tristan trying to talk him out of it."

"Damn him!" Melanie snarled. "What business is it of his what his lord does?"

"It concerns him and the others too because of the coin they hope to gain," Kallie reminded her.

"And does Tristan think de Brock will gain more from a

forced wedding than from a ransom?"

"He does."

Melanie clenched her hands into fists. "If I have gone through all this for naught—"

"Do not make threats, I beg you. You are in no position to do so," Kallie cautioned her.

Melanie walked over to the window in frustration. She had been certain their plan would work. De Brock had not shown signs of wanting anything to do with her since that night in the great hall.

"I cannot allow him to force me into marriage. Not now. Not after Merick and I have known one another. Surely de Brock would not want me now that I am no longer a virgin."

Kallie pondered this new dilemma. "I do not know. It could work to your advantage, but then again, it might just enrage him."

Melanie felt a tremor of fear engulf her. "Enrage him?"

"Aye, for you would have cheated him out of that which he feels is his."

Anger replaced Melanie's fear. "It was not his! He is not my betrothed. Merick and I discussed this at length last night after we...you know. Anyway, we decided if de Brock should discover what I had done, I would say I had been with my betrothed *before* I was stolen."

"That is an idea," Kallie agreed. "Then he would wonder if any issue he may beget is of his loins."

"Exactly."

"Another reason for him to not want you."

"Yes!" Melanie didn't want to consider that he may just wait until he was certain she was not with child before he opted to wed her.

"Plus, I do not think he would suspect anyone would dare to come near you here."

"No, no one would dare, for he has claimed me as his future bride."

Kallie nodded in agreement. "That, and the fact of how hideous you are."

Melanie didn't pay attention to Kallie's last remark because she had climbed up to peek out the window. "Are those not Fontleroy's men out there again?" she asked, concerned that the foolish man was again attempting to call out Dragon.

Kallie dragged a chair over to the window beside Melanie, squinting to see what she was looking at. A light fog still clung to the ground, which the sun had not yet chased away, obscuring her vision. "Where do you see them?"

"Just there, by the edge of the forest. Do they not wear the green surcoats?"

"Aye, they do. But I— Wait, now I see them. They are trying to hide out in the woods. They are spying on Tenebrous!" Kallie couldn't believe the gall and the stupidity of them. They seemed to think it a game to continue to ride to the edge of the forest and wait for Dragon's knights to chase them away.

"Surely de Brock's knights will spot them and ride out?"

"They always do." Kallie looked about the yard. The height they were at gave them the advantage to view much of the castle grounds. The sentries who watched from the parapet also had this advantage. If they spotted anything suspicious, they would give the signal to sound the alarm. The barracks were in their sight, and even as Kallie was peering down, the alarm sounded.

"Good. They have been spotted. See the men there rushing out?" Kallie pointed out the building to Melanie.

"Aye. Good. It's frightening that Fontleroy and his men

skulk around out there like thieves. Especially because when Merick does finally decide to take his leave, he may have to get past them." She shuddered with the thought.

The pair watched the men wait while their horses were brought forward and the soldiers prepared to ride out. It was difficult to tell how many of Fontleroy's men were out there, but it appeared de Brock had instructed the men to take a larger force this time. Usually, when the enemy was spotted, only a dozen soldiers would ride out to chase them off. But this time, at least a dozen knights and a score of men-at-arms were making ready to depart. Melanie was impressed with the speed in which the men prepared themselves and their horses. They were well equipped with swords and shields, and there was a fellow with a bow.

A bow! Melanie gasped suddenly. "Kallie! Look there."

"Where? What is it?"

"That man, the one with the bow. I think it's Merick."

Kallie tried to see who Melanie was pointing at. Finally, her eyes settled on a man who appeared slightly unsure of what he should be doing. With the others hurrying to ready themselves, they seemed either unaware of him or unconcerned. The man, who she was now quite certain was Merick, had secured himself a horse and was mounting.

"He will get himself killed! How could de Brock allow this?" Melanie demanded.

"He must not know," Kallie said grimly.

Melanie jumped down from the chair. "We must tell him then!"

Kallie jumped down too and began heading toward the door. When Melanie began to follow her, Kallie stopped her. "Nay! You must stay here."

"But why? I can help!"

"If my lord sees you running toward him, he will run in the other direction. And then, once he realizes you no longer limp, he will stop. Then he will see your teeth are not missing, for you are not wearing the sap. You would then have much explaining to do!"

Melanie was shocked with her thoughtlessness. She could have blown her cover and risked Merick's life with her haste. "You're right. But please, please hurry. Make him go after Merick. He is not yet ready for battle."

"I will," Kallie assured her, then sped out the door.

~*~

"My lord! My lord!" Kallie yelled as she burst into the solar.

Dragon watched with amusement while Kallie doubled over, trying to catch her breath. "Was there something you wished?" he asked. He was seated before a large wooden desk going over the accounts.

"The player! He…he has gone out…with the others to meet Fontleroy's men!" she finally gasped out.

Dragon was on his feet in an instant and rushing to the door. "Damn that impetuous fool!" he growled, striding down the hallway while Kallie hurried to keep up. They were soon rushing down the flights of stairs and past the great hall. Dragon burst through the double doors and began yelling orders.

"Bring me my horse!" One of his men, seeing the murderous glare on his lord's face, had anticipated the order to bring forth his sword, and he handed de Brock the weapon. Dragon reached down to check that his dagger still rested in his boot and then pulled on his gloves.

Kallie stood close by him while he prepared to ride out. "Do you think we are too late?" she asked anxiously.

A groom was bringing his horse into the yard, and Dragon regarded her grimly before he walked away. "Pray that I am not."

~*~

Merick stayed to the back of the group of men, hopeful no one would notice he had tagged along. He knew he risked much, but he had not been able to control his rage when he'd heard Fontleroy's soldiers were lurking in the forest. The faces of the players, his friends, had flashed in his mind, and he had tasted the bitterness of revenge. The force of his anger had overtaken his good sense. When the alarm was sounded, and the men prepared to ride out, Merick hadn't thought twice to join them. But now, as they neared the enemy, he was beginning to rethink his rashness.

Fontleroy's soldiers heard the horses and looked to see the riders fast approaching. Though they were outnumbered, they did not appear overly concerned, for this was a game they had played many times. The trick was to bait the men out of the castle and allow them to get just close enough. Then they would scatter into the woods, exiting soon after, off to the side, and return to Hatchel Castle.

Ever since encountering the trap they'd been led into, the men of Tenebrous only chased Fontleroy's men until they went into the forest, not bothering to give chase. Dragon had given the order after the deadly attack to hold back and no longer pursue the enemy. By doing so, it would give them a false sense of security. He wanted them to believe they were safe, and the men of Tenebrous were too wary to follow them into the woods again. In the weeks passed since the attack, Fontleroy's men had taken perverse pleasure in baiting Dragon's men, confident they could ride to safety unchallenged.

This time, however, things would go differently.

Dragon, along with Tristan and Holden, had come up

with a plan that would send half their riders into the forest to chase down the men. But the rest would ride around the edge of the forest and wait for the men to sneak out at the other side. The distance was much shorter to go through the forest, so Dragon's men would have to move quickly. Merick, remembering the plan, realized he was probably not yet ready to clash with the enemy in full-out battle, so he decided he would head into the woods to give chase.

Unfortunately, he was not riding at the front of the group, and when they broke into two, he reluctantly had to follow the others or face exposure. It took several minutes of hard riding to get to the edge of the forest, where they expected the enemy to emerge. The men spaced themselves strategically so they could easily converge when the time came. Their presence would be unexpected, and with the other half of their team chasing the enemy from behind, Fontleroy's men would have no choice but to fight.

Merick felt the familiar knot of fright in his belly as he waited for the battle to begin. He sat atop his horse at the farthest end of the string of men. They had drawn their swords and waited with anticipation while Merick was woefully unprepared. He had not thought to bring along a sword, for he did not have one of his own. He had practiced and felt confident enough that given a chance, he could wield one with considerable skill, thanks to the relentless training Dragon had forced him to endure the past several days. But now, all he had was his bow. He pulled it forward from where it rested on his shoulder and reached back to his quiver of arrows. Setting his arrow in place, he took a few steadying deep breaths.

The enemy was approaching. He could hear them crashing through the woods. Fontleroy's men burst through the forest.

Upon sight of the awaiting knights and men-at-arms, they pulled back on their mounts. Though it was only seconds, it felt like time stood still as they hesitated. Then they looked back, and seeing they were pursued, the men reluctantly charged ahead, swords drawn, knowing they had no choice. All hell broke loose as the men of Tenebrous rode forward to meet them. The clash shook the ground as horses thundered toward each other, and steel contacted steel.

Merick did not hesitate but began to pick off the soldiers he could clearly takedown. There were slightly over a score of the enemy, and to their credit, the men gave a good showing of their might.

But they were no match for Dragon's men.

Merick watched, feeling a wave of added relief as he saw the rest of Dragon's men break through the forest to join the fray. Now, knowing they were fighting for their lives, Fontleroy's men became frenzied. They had grouped together in the beginning to watch each other's backs and fight as a team, but now they scattered in different directions, leaving every man for himself.

Merick's relief was short-lived when he spotted a man charging toward him with his sword drawn. He reached back for another arrow, knowing he must hurry if he were to stop this man before he reached him.

But all his arrows were spent.

Having no weapon, Merick could only wait helplessly and watch the man approach. He refused to turn and flee and searched his mind for another way he could fight. And then the grim line of his mouth turned into a smile as he recalled Dragon and his brother Desmond. Merick began to ride toward the man.

~*~

Dragon had charged out of the gate and ridden hard after

his men. He'd seen them break into two groups and took a chance the player had gone around the edge of the forest and not entered within. He had been correct with his assumption and been gifted the sight of his quarry at the farthest end of the line. He'd entered onto the scene when the battle was fully engaged, but he had not stopped his horse to join in the fighting. He knew his men could handle the enemy — they needed no help from him. But the player now confronted the possibility of demise when the enemy scattered and ran like the cowards they were, one of them riding directly at him. Dragon was half the length of the field away, and though he was nearing the player, Fontleroy's man was closer. Dragon charged on, watching with dread as the player began to ride forward toward the enemy. No doubt he'd panicked and ridden in the wrong direction.

Merick thought back to that day at the tournament. During the joust, Dragon and Desmond had appeared evenly matched and unable to unhorse each other. But then Dragon had executed a move which had stunned the crowd and given him the edge he desired. He had done something with his leg, Merick recalled. Slipping his right foot out of the stirrup, he saw the move clearly in his mind's eye. Dragon had bent low and spun around backward with his leg extended. Desmond had ridden straight into Dragon's leg, the force of which had unhorsed Desmond....

Merick broke from his daze when he felt the stunning blow of the weight of the enemy, who'd ridden at him, full against his outstretched leg.

"By God!" he yelled, as he steadied himself and retook his seat in the saddle. He'd done it!

Dragon reached the pair just as Fontleroy's man was coming to his senses. He lay there, stunned upon the ground, covered in dirt and dead leaves. When he finally focused his sights, his gaze became shocked as his awakening mind registered danger. Dragon, now unhorsed, stood before him, sword drawn.

Dragon spared the player a glance. "Nice move," he said, eyeing with wonder the trembling man who sat atop his horse smiling crookedly.

"I had a good teacher," Merick told him.

Chapter 16

Melanie saw Merick ride through the gates with the other men. It had been about an hour since she'd seen Dragon tear off on his horse after him. Merick appeared fine from where she stood, peeking around the corner of the hen house. As they rode past her, Melanie saw that not only was Merick well, he appeared radiant. So did the other men. She guessed it meant they'd met with success. Dragon came through the gates last, and instead of his usual grim countenance, a tight smile curved his lips, indicating he was pleased about something. Perhaps Merick had performed well today, and de Brock had not had to save him? Or maybe he did save him — but she didn't think Merick would look so happy if Dragon had.

When it was safe to leave, Melanie hobbled away from her hiding place. She didn't want to return to her lonely tower room, so she set out around the castle grounds instead. Kallie had come back to the tower earlier to tell her that she'd sent Dragon after Merick. Melanie had been anxious to go outside. She'd had the black sap on her teeth, and she'd been grasping her crutch in a death grip, so Kallie had told her to go. She'd also reminded Melanie that if anyone should be anxiously awaiting Merick's return, it should be Bevenly. As much as it angered Melanie, she knew Kallie was right. It would look suspicious if she flew at him the moment he came riding through the gates. She would have to wait until they were alone before she lit into him like she intended to do.

Melanie slowly hobbled in Merick's direction, deliberately keeping her distance. She watched as he handed off his horse to a lad and walk toward the entrance of Tenebrous with the other men. They were loud and boisterous, going on about the skirmish outside the walls. There was much laughter, and Melanie watched in dismay as Bevenly rushed up to join the men. The easy way she sidled up to Merick and slipped beneath his arm left Melanie glaring furiously after them. When they disappeared inside, she couldn't help but follow.

A half-hour later, Kallie exited the kitchen into the back passageway leading to the great hall. She had a pitcher of ale in her hands. It was so full some of it sloshed against the floor as she abruptly halted. "Lady Melanie! Pardon, but I did not see you there."

"Shhh!" Melanie hissed. "I do not want them to know I am here."

It was obvious she was spying on the men in the hall. Kallie peeked through the doorway and saw Merick seated with a group of men, including Dragon, around one of the long tables.

"I am glad to see he is well."

"So am I, so I can kill him myself," snarled Melanie.

Kallie rolled her eyes and set the heavy pitcher on the floor by her feet. "You know he is only playing a part. She means nothing to him."

But even Kallie didn't appear convinced, considering the way Merick allowed Bevenly to cozy up to him. She was practically sitting in his lap. Melanie noticed Dragon was frowning at the young woman. He, too, did not seem pleased with her presence.

"How can he act this way after what we shared last night? Am I so easily dismissed from his mind?"

"Nay, of course not!" Kallie insisted. She picked up the ale. "I must take this in there, but when I come back, we can walk together, all right?"

"All right," Melanie agreed, then sniffled.

Balancing the pitcher on her hip, Kallie made her way over to the men. Dragon was now standing, and the men had quieted to hear what he wanted to say.

"I saw something today on the field of battle, and I was quite impressed," de Brock began. "I saw a man with no weapon being charged by a soldier armed with a sword and deadly intent. Though his odds were few, this man," he nodded in Merick's direction, "Did not flee, as many would."

The men around chorused their agreement.

"Instead, he rode toward the enemy and exercised a difficult maneuver."

The men chuckled at this, for they had seen their lord execute the move at tournaments and even on battlefields before. It was one of many different moves he did that made him stand out from other warriors. Merick, however, swallowed down a lump in his throat and cursed himself for a fool. He had seen Dragon execute the move at Balan Castle, and Dragon had seen Merick perform the same stunt today. Merick had been worried on the ride back to Tenebrous that de Brock would put two and two together and finally recognize Merick, recalling that he was not Reginald but an impostor. He'd been relieved Dragon had not called him out right then and there, but now he was once again fearful.

"Therefore, I wish to present to you, Reginald Finlay, a gift." Tristan placed a sword in de Brock's outstretched hand, and de Brock presented it to Merick.

Bevenly clapped her hands while Merick took the sword, breathing a huge sigh of relief. For a moment there, when Dragon had taken up the sword, he'd been afraid he would smite his head from his shoulders. The others gave up a cheer of congratulations.

"Thank you, my lord," Merick said finally, proudly admiring the weapon.

"And though you have proven you do not need it...." Dragon raised his cup in a toast. "May you never ride unarmed into battle again!"

Kallie was rushing to fill their empty cups with ale, and in her haste, she dumped the pitcher's contents down the back of Bevenly's gown when she leaned over her.

"Oh my!" she gasped, trying to mask her glee with a look of horror. "I am sorry!"

Bevenly jumped to her feet, shuddering from the shock of the chilled ale. Her feet were becoming wet from the puddle around her. "You clumsy fool!"

"Enough!" Dragon said loudly, abruptly ending any further name calling.

Bevenly looked enraged but held her tongue when she saw the look of warning on de Brock's face.

"Let me help you clean up," Kallie offered, but Bevenly just shook her head and hurried from the room. "I will get some more ale, my lord," she said to de Brock, smiling at him conspiratorially. He did not reply but gave her a wink before she turned back toward the kitchen.

When she reached the hall, Melanie hugged her fiercely. "You are the very best of friends!"

~*~

The eve of the last day of August arrived, and with it came a cool breeze lifting the heat of the long summer days. The inhabitants of Tenebrous had taken to the neglected fields outside the walls to bring in what they could. They were grateful to obtain any bounty from the castle's first harvest in a long time. The fields had been choked with overgrown weeds, suffering from so many years lying fallow. It had also been years since the abandoned village had housed any families. Since the old lord of Tenebrous had died without issue, leaving the castle with no master, they had long since fled.

When Jamie de Brock was gifted Tenebrous, he'd been given only slight preparation as to what he faced. He knew the castle sat empty. He also knew the villagers had left, for they could not survive there without a master. But Jamie had not been deterred. He'd never shied away from a challenge, and that was exactly what Tenebrous offered him. Comrades had joined him, homeless fellows like he himself had once been. Dragon offered them a place with him, which was more enjoyable than the life they had expected to live. The plague had wiped out many while they had been fighting in Crecy with Edward's heir. Their return had not been the warm homecoming they'd expected. Instead of returning to their families, many had found themselves to be sole survivors. So they had become family to each other.

Dragon had traveled with Tristan, and since he'd had no family, Tristan had asked him to come home with him. But when they'd arrived, only Tristan's young brother Benton was alive. They'd tried to eke out a living in the devastated village, but then the king had summoned Dragon. He'd traveled to see Edward alone, but after receiving Tenebrous from the grateful king for aiding his son in battle, Dragon had gone back for Tristan and Benton. Together, the three of them had ridden through other villages, gathering men they'd fought with and what was left of their families, and brought them to Tenebrous.

Jamie had taken possession of his castle in the late fall. They'd just barely survived the harsh winter with the supplies they'd brought with them. The next spring, he'd been forced to leave to enter into tournaments to win coin. It was his hope to restore Tenebrous to its former glory and then to recover the village as well. Slowly things had been turning around, and besides the odd problem here or there, Jamie felt certain they'd be well secure before the winter arrived.

Tonight, the air was cool enough to warrant a fire, and the hearth in the great hall crackled its warmth all through supper. Merick sat at the long table with a group of men who were quiet tonight. Usually, dinner was a boisterous affair, but the day had been exceptionally long and hard, with everyone spending time preparing the gathered harvest for storage. Each of them took on many tasks, and several did things that were considered women's work, like smoking meat to see them through the winter months and making candles and soap. Jamie had overseen the work and was impressed with the knowledge each person brought to his group. One day soon, Jamie had promised them, there would be dozens of women at Tenebrous, and the men would only have to concern themselves with hunting and fighting.

Despite his exhaustion, Merick had enjoyed the break from the rigorous training Dragon usually had them doing. He'd been surprised how much work went into creating things he'd always taken for granted. When the first signs of winter began, they would be well prepared. But then Merick remembered he had planned to be long gone by then. Instead of feeling happy about leaving, he was surprised the thought no longer warmed him as it once had. It was strange, Merick reflected. He no longer considered Dragon his enemy. Since the man showed no interest in Melanie, he no longer seemed a threat to them. And the other fellows had become like brothers to him. It stunned Merick when he suddenly realized he did not want to leave.

What did life at Balan Castle offer him compared to life at Tenebrous? Certainly, he had his family and his comforts. But here, he had respect. The men considered him one of them. They were not cruel and did not belittle him constantly, which was almost a daily occurrence back home. Why could he not just stay here? But then Melanie's sweet face flashed before his eyes. She was so lovely. He could not expect her to continue to hobble around toothless and shunned so he may remain.

After dinner, Merick turned down an offer to join the men for games and drinks. He returned to his room and sat down on his bed. Looking around, he was reminded of the luxury still bestowed upon him as an honored guest. De Brock should have moved him into the barracks by now with the other soldiers, but Merick surmised he must have simply forgotten. The man did have a lot on his mind considering all he had to deal with. It was no easy task running a castle, especially one as neglected as Tenebrous had been. And now that tournament season was over, de Brock had no other way to gather coin.

It was strange, considering it looked like de Brock was not going to force the union with Melanie, that he had not ransomed her yet. It had been Melanie's plan all along, and Merick had to admit it was a good one. She had succeeded in revolting Dragon to the point he practically fled in the opposite direction whenever she came near.

Merick did not understand what it was Dragon waited for. Obviously, he desired Kallie, and all the men understood she belonged to their lord. None trifled with her, even teasingly. In fact, the men respected her greatly, which was strange considering she was only a servant. But no matter how Dragon felt about Kallie, she was still a penniless maid. Wedding her would not bring him the coin he desired. So why would de Brock continue to keep Melanie a prisoner here? The thought confused him, for it would seem the logical thing to do was ransom her. Unless he had an alternative course of action planned? Perhaps he thought to give her to one of his men as a boon? Tristan perhaps?

Merick couldn't help but chuckle a little when the image of Tristan's face if he were to be gifted Melanie as his bride entered his mind. Tristan would no doubt wonder what it was he had done to annoy his lord to deserve such punishment. Merick laughed out loud but then reined in his amusement. He should be ashamed of himself. Here he was enjoying his friend's imagined misfortune and at the cost of his betrothed. As he turned his thoughts to Melanie, Merick smiled again.

Last night had been magical to him. Never could he have imagined Melanie so passionate. Her body responded to his touch as though she were made just for his pleasure. And indeed, his enjoyment had been great. But he knew by Melanie's cry of satisfaction she, too, had enjoyed their lovemaking. She had made him feel so powerful, so masculine. Perhaps his overinflated ego had also been one of the things which made him act so rashly this morning. It was true he had been angry, but too, he had felt invincible. It had just been lucky for him he had executed Dragon's move so flawlessly. It was also lucky Dragon had been there ready with his sword when the man had regained his senses after being knocked to the ground.

All of Fontleroy's men at the battle today who had been rounded up had been tied securely together and returned to Hatchel Castle on foot. Merick had at first wondered about the intention Dragon had in letting the men go with only a stern warning for their lord, but after seeing their humiliation, he realized the wisdom in the act. The men would think twice before they set out on such a venture again. Besides, de Brock had not been so kind as to return their horses or weapons. When they returned to bury their dead, it would also serve as a reminder to them not to underestimate their opponent.

Merick retired for the night, thinking of Melanie. He was tempted to sneak up to her room so they may be together again, but he dared not risk it. It wasn't just getting caught that frightened him—more so, it was the thought of getting her with child. If things did not go as planned, and they were not able to escape Tenebrous before the winter months set in, Melanie could find herself in an awkward predicament. It was true she could say she'd been with her betrothed before Dragon took her, but how would Melanie feel about being with child before she was actually married? He did not think she would be pleased, nor would her parents, if she returned home in such a condition. Technically, they were betrothed to one another, which was practically being married in the eyes of God. But they had not actually said their vows to one another. Too, Merick had released Melanie from their betrothal before she had been taken. In her eyes, she may feel they were no longer betrothed. She may feel ashamed about what they had done.

Merick suddenly sat upright in bed. He had not talked to Melanie today. He had not even seen her. It could be she was upset about what they had done last night. Tomorrow, Merick decided as he lay back down, he would find her and make things right. He would make certain she did not suffer any regrets. If she did, he would reassure her that he was wrong to break their betrothal, and he truly had not meant it. That should ease any concerns she may be suffering from, Merick assured himself, as he contentedly drifted off to sleep.

~*~

Merick heard her laughter before he caught sight of Melanie in the garden the next morning. He had slipped out after breakfast before he was to join the men for sword training with the intention of setting things right with her. Spotting her hobbling off in the direction of the garden, he had slowly trailed behind, not wanting to make it obvious he was following. But it seemed he had arrived too late, for, by the sound of it, Melanie was not alone. Merick cautiously approached and peered through the bushes at a resting place with a bench set amongst the roses. Here he spotted his betrothed sitting closely with a young fellow he recognized as one of de Brock's squires. Samuel was his name if Merick remembered correctly. Instead of making his presence known, Merick instead decided to remain where he was. It would not do well to have this young fellow tell others he and Melanie had a conversation in the garden, even if it seemed like a chance encounter.

"Have those young men bothered you again, Samuel?" Melanie asked her companion. She had been amazed to see when coming upon him sitting there on the bench that a beautiful butterfly perched on his finger. Slowly she'd approached, careful to not startle the insect, and taken a seat beside him. They'd remained silent for a few moments, and then Samuel had sneezed quite suddenly, and the butterfly had flown away.

"I have been holding that in for a while," Samuel had sheepishly admitted, causing Melanie to laugh out loud. He now regarded her shyly and smiled. "Nay, not since the other day. I think they may be worried you might approach them again."

"I'm glad. I guess," Melanie said. She had spotted some of the fellows wandering around the castle grounds, but they had given her a wide berth.

"Why do others fear you so?"

"You mean other than because of my beautiful smile?" she said dryly.

He was regarding her intriguingly. "I hardly noticed."

"You are sweet, but it is not only my mouth that makes them run away. If you have not noticed, I also walk strangely."

"No stranger than some," Samuel said.

Melanie sighed. "It is because of my smell," she told him with embarrassment. It would now only be a matter of moments before her new friend would surely make his excuses to leave her presence.

Samuel leaned closer and sniffed the air around her. "I detect no odor."

"Well, I do not actually smell right now, but I did when I applied specially treated bandages to my leg."

"Ah, that explains it."

"I am afraid I have scared off most people around here," Melanie said.

"It must be lonely for you."

Melanie looked away, so Samuel could not see the sudden tears that rushed to her eyes. His kindness was sincere, and she appreciated it. She looked back at him when she had her emotions under control. "It is lonely."

Merick almost leapt out from his hiding place when Samuel reached to take Melanie's hand in his. But, unbeknownst to him was the fact that while he was spying on Melanie and Samuel, he was also being watched. Bevenly had spied him going into the garden, and she had followed. When she saw him stop and peek through the bushes, she had hidden behind a tree and waited. She was close enough to faintly make out the sound of a man and a woman's voice, and she surmised from the way Merick was acting, it must be Melanie. From the look on his face and the way he was clenching his fists, it appeared he was going to make his presence known to the pair.

Just as he was about to step from the bushes, Bevenly rushed forward and latched her arm through his. When Melanie and Samuel looked up, it appeared that Merick and Bevenly had arrived together.

Merick had been startled when he felt someone grab onto his arm, and he had almost shaken himself free. But he caught sight of the dainty hand and was able to control his reaction. Bevenly had smiled up at him sweetly but warningly, and as they stepped into the clearing, she said, "Oh, what a lovely spot, is it not *Reginald*?" Her meaning was clear — she expected him to play along with her.

"Aye," Merick replied. "But it seems we are not alone." He looked pointedly at Melanie and then turned his gaze on Samuel.

Melanie could not help but see the anger in his look. If she didn't know him better, she might have jumped to the conclusion he was upset about having been caught taking a romantic stroll with another woman, but he wasn't. It was obvious by the way he was sizing up Samuel that Merick was practically boiling over with jealously.

Bevenly could see it too. She had wanted to reinforce her hold over Merick, and what better way than to flaunt their presence in front of Melanie? But her plan was going awry. Merick didn't seem concerned in the least that she could expose him as a fraud. He seemed only concerned about finding his beloved Melanie with another man.

"Let us away, Reginald," Bevenly said, tugging gently on his arm. Merick seemed loath to leave, but finally, he relented.

"Fine," he practically spat. He had seen the fearful look on Melanie's face, and he knew she was terrified he would reveal his identity as her betrothed. And indeed, he had almost been ready to do so. The selfishness of the act had not surpassed him, though, and he had reined in his anger. It would do neither he nor Melanie any good to reveal himself to Samuel, even though it would have given him supreme pleasure to see the look on the man's face.

Melanie watched as Merick turned his back and began stomping away, pulling Bevenly along with him. She watched them until they were out of sight. Samuel's voice interrupted her tremulous thoughts, and she finally turned her attention back to him.

"Do you know that man?" he asked.

"I have seen him around the castle," Melanie said, trying to appear unconcerned.

"He is that player everyone is talking about. It is said he is a hero and single-handedly killed five men and saved some of de Brock's own knights."

"Oh, was that he?" Melanie tried to sound impressed.

"Aye, but I wonder what he was so furious about? He looked like he wanted to throttle me right here in the garden."

"He must have just been angered to have his stroll interrupted."

"Perhaps," Samuel agreed, though he was not quite convinced.

Now that the moment of danger had passed, Melanie

began to feel pleased about the way things had turned out. Bevenly's attempts at making her feel insecure about her and Merick's relationship had backfired. His only concern had been that Melanie was alone with a handsome young man in the garden. And as for Merick, it served him right to be upset. After the way he had ignored her yesterday, and for all the other times he had been too busy training with Dragon's men to pay her any mind, he'd had it coming to him. It was payback time.

Melanie smiled and tucked her hand in the crook of Samuel's arm. "How about we take a stroll?"

Chapter 17

It had been three days since that morning in the garden. Three days filled with Melanie spending time making Merick see she was a force to be reckoned with. No longer would she sit idly by while he trained and frolicked with the enemy. No longer would she wait for him to throw her a tidbit of his time. She no longer acted as though she was desperate for a glimpse of him. She put on a good show of independence and indifference. But little did he know, she still spent her nights craving his touch. He had not returned to her room since the one time they had shared their passion. His dismissive attitude bothered her, but it was less painful since she had found another to share her time with.

Young Samuel was everything Merick was not—thoughtful and kind, considerate of her feelings, and eager to please her—the way Merick used to be. Melanie had shamelessly flaunted her friendship with Samuel. She'd enjoyed the way Merick's eyes turned to fire, burning into them whenever they passed him by. Blissfully unaware of the animosity his presence created, Samuel went about his days ignorant of the fact he was being used. Melanie had not felt overly bad about her behavior, for Samuel gained much from their union. Besides truly enjoying their time together, he was no longer bullied. The other young squires feared Melanie far too much to want to cause her to seek them out for a reprimand.

At first, Melanie's intention had been solely to cause Merick jealousy, the way she had been jealous of Bevenly. But since that day, when she had seen the truth in Merick's eyes — that she was everything to him and that Bevenly was merely a distraction — Melanie had regained her confidence. It was strange to think how Samuel had brought about her contentment, even if it had been in a roundabout way. He'd accomplished something that even an act of intimacy between her and Merick had failed to do.

But then something changed.

It went from being a game to being something quite serious. The emotions emanating from Samuel were hard to decipher. Certainly, they were friends, but Melanie feared he was beginning to feel something more. He had not voiced his feelings, nor had he ever done more than hold her hand, but Melanie sensed he desired more than friendship from her. Even worse, Merick now turned away whenever he saw them. He had gone from being angry to not caring. That hurt the most. Perhaps her plan had backfired. Perhaps Merick no longer cared what she did with her time or whom she spent it with.

Melanie hobbled pensively around the yard, deep in thought. She barely heard Samuel's approach, and he had to speak her name twice before she turned to him. "Oh, I'm sorry, I was distracted."

Samuel smiled sweetly. "Is it something I can help you figure out?"

"Nay, it's nothing." Melanie turned onto the garden path, and Samuel trailed faithfully behind her.

"It is a fine day, unlike yesterday," he observed.

"Aye, though the sun shone, the wind was too brisk for my liking."

Samuel studied the sky for a moment. "I think the weather will hold today, but tonight it shall be cool."

"It seems to be getting colder and colder at night. I had to put an extra blanket on my bed and build up the fire before retiring."

The corner of Samuel's mouth turned down in a frown. "Lord de Brock should move you from that drafty tower and into one of the rooms below."

Melanie nodded her head in agreement, but his words gave her cause to consider Dragon's intentions. Perhaps him not moving her was a good sign. Perhaps he thought, *why bother* if he was only planning on ransoming her. But then again, maybe he just planned on keeping her a prisoner in the tower forever. If she was speaking to Merick, she could ask him, but she wasn't.

"I'm sorry, I didn't mean to give you any unpleasant thoughts."

Melanie walked over and sat down on the bench they had shared before. She patted the spot beside her, and Samuel sat down. "I'm not going to worry about Dragon's plans for me. I'm sure I'll find out soon enough."

Samuel shuddered a little. He did not like to think about Lord de Brock, for the man frightened him. But as much as he worried about Melanie's fate, Samuel knew she had nothing to fear. Even if the man decided to keep her, he would never be cruel. It was true he was huge and formidable, but Samuel had to admit, he'd never seen him harm anyone small or helpless—

especially not a woman or a child. He did yell a lot, but only at other men.

"I find it amusing how the others still flee whenever you come near," he said to distract her from worrying.

"Yes, amusing," Melanie agreed, although she failed to find any enjoyment in the thought anymore.

"I know it must be lonely for you sometimes, but you still have Kallie and me as your friends. And you must admit how silly it is that the others have yet to realize you do not smell anymore."

"They do not get close enough to find out."

Samuel laughed. "And your teeth...," he howled.

It had been quite by accident Samuel had discovered Melanie's little ruse with the black sap in her mouth. He'd offered her a sweet he had saved from dinner, and when Melanie had bit into the morsel, the sap had become stuck on it. She'd quickly explained how she'd wanted to make herself unattractive to de Brock and begged Samuel not to expose her. Samuel had, of course, agreed to go along with her game. She had not been quite brave enough to let on that her limp was also faked. Kallie's part in her little deception was also not revealed.

They talked pleasantly for a while longer until Kallie came upon them. "Oh, there you are, my lady! I have looked all over for you." Samuel did not know Kallie was actually a lady — only Melanie was privy to that bit of information. So in others' company, Kallie continued to play the part of a humble servant.

Melanie stood up at once, concerned over the distressed look on her friend's face. "What is it?"

"My lord wishes to see you in the solar at once," Kallie said.

Samuel and Melanie both gasped. Melanie had known

this moment was coming, but she was still unprepared. Kallie came forward and took her arm, urging her to hurry. There was no time to even ponder the possibilities of what it was de Brock had decided. Melanie said a hasty goodbye to Samuel, who in turn wished her luck, then she hurried off toward the castle with Kallie.

"What has he decided?" Melanie hissed as they rushed down the garden path.

"I don't know. He has not confided in me."

The tone of Kallie's voice betrayed her anxiousness, and Melanie was too fearful to ask more questions. A few minutes later, Kallie deposited her at the solar door. She announced her arrival, gave Melanie's hand a squeeze, then fled.

Melanie stepped forward when de Brock beckoned her to enter. Every footstep seemed to weigh her down. She remembered to limp, and this slowed her progress toward him even more.

Dragon stood by the cold hearth, leaning casually against the stone mantle. He was dressed all in black, his usual garb, the look on his handsome face unreadable. He held a cup in his hand filled with ale, and the tips of his fingers were stained with ink. A heavy wooden desk littered with parchment stood near to him, and it looked like he had taken a moment out of his busy schedule to decide what to do with her.

Melanie remembered when he had captured her in the forest. He had chased her and held her in his muscular arms. Then he had kissed her. No one had ever kissed her like that before, and the memory of it made her shiver suddenly. What did he want of her? Surely he did not want her for his bride? He was dashingly handsome and could not possibly want a toothless cripple for his wife. De Brock was watching her approach, and she saw a moment of unease cross his face. He lifted his head and sniffed the air, but when he failed to smell the horrendous scent, he appeared relieved.

Finally, she stood before him. Dragon thought she would never get there, and he was anxious to have this meeting over with. He could tell by the look on Melanie's face she was terrified of what he was going to say. Other things had been on his mind, and he knew he should have dealt with her earlier or at least informed her of his intentions. It had taken a gentle reminder from Kallie that Melanie still did not know what he wanted of her and how anxious she was. But he had decided her fate. He would tell her of his plan to release her because taking her as his bride was completely out of the question. He hoped his decision would bring her some peace of mind, for he did not wish her ill. The thought of her leaving his castle and having things get back to normal pleased him. His men had voiced complaints about her presence, and they would be happy to see her finally on her way.

"I know you must be wondering about your fate," Dragon began. He had consciously gentled his voice, knowing he had a tendency to growl when he talked. Melanie was giving him her undivided attention, which pleased him — he did not want to have to repeat himself. "When I first brought you here to Tenebrous, I had the intention of making you my bride."

Melanie nodded her head, acknowledging what he said.

"I had intended to wed you, but my conscience has overcome my rashness. I was desperate, you see, for coin. I was not thinking clearly, and I fear I have acted abominably. I...I apologize."

She was struck dumb. She attempted to smile at least to let him know she accepted his apology, but then she realized he was watching her mouth with trepidation. Quickly, she ducked her head.

"'Tis all right, my lord. I understand, and I accept your apology," she mumbled.

"Thank you."

Melanie wondered if he was finished with her, for he remained silent. She hazarded a look up at him, and he seemed to be contemplating something.

"Ah, yes," he said finally. "I have decided to return you home."

"You…. You are not going to ransom me?"

This was not the reaction he was expecting. He expected thanks, relief, perhaps even a kiss of gratitude. Why was she questioning him?

"Nay. Your family has suffered enough from my thoughtlessness."

"But, my lord, if you return me home without demanding ransom, I will be ruined!"

"I have not touched you!"

"Everyone will think you have and have found me wanting."

Dragon was frustrated. This was not going the way he had planned.

"If a ransom is demanded, then they would expect you are offering me to be returned unharmed and *intact* in exchange for a sum," Melanie explained.

"So you want me to ransom you?" Dragon said, exasperated.

"Aye! My family will pay dearly to have me back. You will have your coin, and my reputation shall be spared."

Dragon was wondering if he might have to pay them to take her back. This was the most irritating conversation he had ever had.

"Then I will ransom you, my lady, if that is what you wish," he accented. "I shall send a man out at first light tomorrow with a note."

"Thank you, my lord." Melanie did smile at him this time and took perverse delight when she saw him cringe.

~*~

"Guess what? Guess what?" Melanie hollered as she rushed back toward the garden and saw Samuel. He was still seated but quickly took to his feet when he noticed her return.

"It must be good news for you to be smiling so."

Checking to make sure no one else was nearby, Melanie pulled the sap from her teeth and held it in the palm of her hand. So caught up with excitement, she flung herself into Samuel's arms.

"He is going to ransom me!"

"Is he? Well now, what fine news," Samuel told her, although he did not feel any joy from her announcement. He knew it was selfish of him, but he did not wish for her to leave.

"He is sending a man out tomorrow with the note."

"That is wonderful!" Kallie said.

Melanie and Samuel pulled quickly away from each other when they heard Kallie's voice. "Kallie! I did not hear you," Melanie said, clutching the sap tightly. She would have to be more careful over the next little while. She was lucky this time it was only her friend who had seen her—her carelessness could have ruined everything.

Kallie came forward and hugged Melanie tightly. "I shall miss you, my lady."

It suddenly dawned on Melanie she would be leaving. She would be glad to be away from Tenebrous, where she had to constantly put on an act, but she would miss her friends. "I wish you could come with me."

"You know I cannot leave him," Kallie whispered.

"But he will not wed you—" Melanie began, heartsick over her friend's predicament.

"Hush now." Kallie stopped her with a finger to her lips. "Please, let us speak of it no more."

Melanie remembered they were not alone—Samuel was still in the garden. She turned to him and saw the forlorn look upon his face. Before she could say anything more, Samuel began to walk away.

"I must return to the yard. They will be looking for me. I have been gone too long," he said.

Melanie could see he was upset. She did not want to embarrass him by making a fuss about it. "I will see you later, then."

He nodded, and then he was gone.

Kallie turned to her. "He is falling for you. You know that, don't you?"

"Aye."

"It will hurt him less when you leave if you stop spending so much time together now."

Melanie knew she was right. "I will miss his friendship, but I will try to stay away."

"I think that is wise."

Neither of them were aware they weren't alone in the garden. Beverly had seen Melanie quickly hobble to seek out Samuel, and she had followed her discreetly. She'd watched the pair embrace, only to be interrupted by Kallie's arrival. Their faces had been flushed from embarrassment to be caught in such an intimate act.

She'd watched them over the past few days, seeing them

become closer and friendlier. Of course, Melanie was only trying to make Merick jealous, but he was aware of what she was doing. Her plan seemed to backfire because Merick was no longer acting like a jealous lover. Now he was just angry.

His reaction had given Bevenly hope. She wanted him for herself, and if Melanie and Samuel became involved in truth, then perhaps she would get her wish. Indeed, it appeared that Melanie was frustrated with Merick's behavior, and even Bevenly had to admit she couldn't blame her. He was infuriating. He'd thrown himself into training, and when he wasn't on the field attacking his opponent with vigor, he was dicing and drinking with the lord's men. It was quite strange he should act this way when he was supposed to be there to free Melanie from de Brock's capture.

Merick no longer seemed concerned that Melanie was spending so much time with another man either, even if he knew she was only doing it to make him jealous. A woman who was being ignored by her betrothed could be a dangerous thing. Left to her own devices, there was no telling how far Melanie was willing to go. She just might decide to take her little charade to the next step. And Melanie couldn't have chosen a more suitable match, Bevenly conceded. Samuel was every woman's dream — sweet and kind, considerate and doting, not to mention handsome. Perhaps those traits were the very reason Melanie was so drawn to him — he no doubt reminded her of how Merick used to be.

Bevenly strolled back through the garden toward the yard when she saw Melanie and Kallie leave. She had just barely made out what Melanie had been saying, noting it had something to do with a meeting with Lord de Brock. She had been excited about something, so it was probably good news for Melanie. She thought she'd heard Melanie say something about being ransomed. De Brock wouldn't take her to wife, it was rumored because of the spill she'd taken down the stairs. He no longer found her attractive. Now Melanie walked with a limp and had no front teeth, and she also stunk terribly. De Brock needed coin, so it would only make sense he would want to ransom her to make some money. Especially after all the trouble he'd gone through to take her. It was a shame he was too shallow to marry her. It would have solved all of Bevenly's problems. Then she could have Merick, and they would remain here at Tenebrous, as she knew Merick wanted to do. He was happy here, it seemed. The other men liked and respected him, unlike back at Balan Castle, where he complained of being the brunt of everyone's jokes.

Bevenly liked it here as well. She'd become used to living in the castle over the past few weeks, it being the longest she'd ever remained in one place in over ten years. Traveling with the players, who'd been like a family to her, was all she'd known for so long. But now they were no longer alive, and it was time to think about what she wanted to do with her life. When she thought about it, alone in the little alcove she'd been given to sleep, Bevenly knew she was ready to settle down. She wanted a husband, someone to share her life with, and children. She no longer wanted to roam from place to place with nowhere to call home.

But if de Brock were ready to ransom Melanie, it meant she would soon be leaving. Merick would have no reason to stay on. Despite being angry with her about Samuel, he would still go after Melanie when she left. He would give no thought to leaving, and she would be alone again. But at least she would still be at Tenebrous. Of course, if Merick left and asked her to join him—which didn't seem likely, as much as he reassured her he would—she would go with him. Perhaps she could find a place for herself at Balan Castle. Bevenly sighed with defeat. Deep down, she knew Merick would never be hers. If he asked her to go after Melanie with him, she would refuse. Her chances for happiness at Tenebrous were greater than they would be chasing after a man who was in love with someone else. At Balan Castle, she would be more of an outcast than Merick ever was.

Chapter 18

Merick heard the news about Melanie that night. He was in the barracks with the other men when Holden relayed the information to the group. Some of the men had cheered with relief at the mention of her ransom, while others had laughed. They'd all known their lord would not consider marrying the girl—it was just too unlikely to imagine. They'd even made jokes about him trying to bed her on their wedding night if he'd gone through with it. "He'd have to wear a blindfold," one man had said. "And do the deed with one hand while the other plugged his nose!" laughed another. The endless jokes had plagued Merick. After all, this was his betrothed they were talking about. He knew they were only having fun, and eventually, he'd laughed despite his discomfort.

All the implications of the announcement occurred to Merick at once. This was what they had been waiting for, he'd thought excitedly—at first. Melanie's plan to make the Dragon return her home had worked. Soon, after she was safely gone, he could make his own escape. He would wait a few days and then announce that he and Bevenly had decided to leave. Although the thought of making the trek home with Bevenly was unsettling, he knew he must honor his promise to bring her along. He would worry about her presence when he returned to Balan Castle. Perhaps his mother could find a use for her, he wondered. Besides, he and Melanie would soon be settled in Hadley Castle after they wed.

But then another thought hit him.

He would no longer be at Tenebrous, nor could he ever return. He would miss the others, he realized, especially Tristan and Holden. Hell, he would even miss Jamie de Brock, the legendary Dragon—the man he was willing to challenge for Melanie. He had learned so much in his time here. When he returned home, everyone would soon see he was not the man they remembered. He smiled when he thought about the alehouse scoundrels who had endlessly plagued him. They would certainly be in for a big surprise when he returned.

"It is good news, no?" Tristan's question brought him back from his reverie.

"Yes, good news. I hope he gets a fortune for her," Merick replied.

"As long as they pay before they see her, he'll do all right. If it's after, then perhaps not," a fellow remarked.

"Unless they do the exchange with a bag over her head, and as long as she doesn't have to walk far to a waiting horse. That could take her all day!"

"What happens when she gets within smelling distance?"

Questions, comments, and more jokes at Melanie's expense flew around the room. Merick chuckled, pretending to be enjoying the game like the others, but it dawned on him just how much Melanie had put herself through. Her plan had succeeded in turning Dragon away from her, but at a cost. She was an outcast here. It was no wonder she was so anxious to leave. Merick felt badly—his behavior toward her lately hadn't been too kind either. He had been so caught up in becoming a warrior and fitting in with the Tenebrous knights, he had sorely neglected her. She did have Kallie's friendship, but Kallie was occupied most of the time with her duties throughout the day, leaving Melanie to her own devices. It wasn't any wonder she'd gone so far as to make him jealous with young Samuel. It must have been very lonely for her.

It was late, and he was tempted to climb the tower stairs to make peace with Melanie, but he was hesitant to leave the men. He knew it was selfish of him, but considering the late hour, he would rather enjoy their company right now. It wouldn't be too much longer before he was gone. He had the rest of his life to make things up to Melanie.

~*~

Kallie picked up the breakfast tray from Melanie's room the next morning and found her friend balancing on the chair, looking out the window.

"What are you doing?" she asked.

"Looking for Samuel," Melanie replied without turning around.

"I thought you were going to try and keep away from him—you know, to let him down easy?"

"That's why I'm looking for him. If I know where he is, I can avoid him," Melanie said.

"Oh. Well, have you spotted him?"

"Not yet. But I don't want to spend the entire day up here. I'll go out of my mind. I'm just going to have to take my chances and hope I don't run into him."

"If you do run into him, you can always make up an excuse to leave," Kallie said.

"I don't want to look obvious. I think he's hurt enough already."

Kallie was thoughtful a moment. "We could always wrap the stinking bandages around your leg. That'll keep him away."

"No thanks! I'd rather take my chances."

"Suit yourself."

Kallie left the room, and Melanie climbed down from the window. She wrapped her cloak around her shoulders and left the room. Perhaps Samuel was training with the other squires, and she could make it out for a quick stroll around the grounds. Once outside, she began a slow trek around the castle. Men were in the yard, as usual, training with swords, and others were in the field with the quintain. Some knights were in the tiltyard practicing the joust. Kallie had told her many of Dragon's knights trained rigorously in preparation for the tournaments in the spring and summer. The coin they earned would supply Tenebrous and their lord with much-needed funds to help run the castle.

Unfortunately, it was never quite enough, Kallie had revealed — hence the desperate need for finding a bride. Melanie almost felt badly she had foiled Dragon's plans. He wasn't such a bad fellow. He had just gone about things the wrong way. He needed to woo a woman with sweet words and gentleness to get what he wanted, not drag her off to his castle like a barbarian. How she wished Kallie would just reveal she was a lady! It would solve Dragon's money woes and Kallie's problem too. What would Kallie do if Dragon brought home another woman to wed? The next one might not be so reviled by the idea, and it would kill Kallie to have to watch Dragon wed someone else.

Melanie sat down on the garden bench. When her mind

wandered, she always seemed to head straight to this location. It was so peaceful and secluded. Here, she could be alone with her thoughts while being surrounded by beauty, which was better than hashing things out in her gloomy tower room.

What if she could convince Kallie to reveal her status to Dragon? She would certainly feel better about leaving her friend if she knew Kallie and de Brock would end up together. It would make leaving so much easier to bear, especially considering how doubtful it was she and Kallie would ever see each other again.

"I see I'm not the only one with a lot on their mind."

Melanie startled when she heard Samuel's voice, for she had failed to hear his approach. Seeing the lost look on her friend's face made her forget all about her resolve to avoid being near him. She patted the seat beside her.

"Come and join me, Samuel. We need to talk."

He came forward like he was approaching the scaffold. "I know," he said, taking a seat beside her.

"I see you're sad, but please, could you try to be just a little bit happy for me?"

Samuel sighed loudly. "I am, really, I am. I know how hard it's been on you here. I just wish things didn't have to end so permanently. I know once you leave, I'll never see you again."

"Are you worried about the other squires bothering you once I'm gone?" Melanie asked.

"No, they haven't bothered me in days. I think they've found someone else to harass."

"I would hate to leave you worrying that they would start in on you again."

"I'm learning how to handle myself quite well. And Holden told me the other day we should be leaving soon."

"Why is Holden leaving?" Melanie was puzzled. Holden

was one of Dragon's most valued men, she thought. Why would he leave Tenebrous?

"Yes, he brought a bunch of us here with him when he came, but he will soon be lord of his own castle," Samuel said.

"I didn't know that. Why would he bring his men here to train?"

"He is his uncle's heir. The man is aging yet still lives and wasn't quite ready to step aside and let him run things yet, so Holden came here so Lord de Brock could help him. He had to learn the machinations of running a castle and all the stuff that goes along with it. I guess his uncle didn't have the time or the inclination to train him. Holden and Lord de Brock have known each other several years, so it only made sense de Brock would help him."

"Oh," Melanie said. "I guess that means we'll both be leaving."

Samuel looked distraught. He reached out and took Melanie's hand in his. "I wish instead we could both remain here, but I know it's not meant to be."

Melanie felt badly for him. She was going home and would marry Merick when he returned—her life was laid out before her. It surprised her she no longer looked toward her future as something to be resigned to. After what she'd been through, all the uncertainties and all the fear, she now embraced her fate. She couldn't wait to become Merick's wife.

Poor Samuel, she thought. He had fancied himself to be falling in love, and now he had to let her go. He was being very brave despite his disappointment. Melanie put her hands on his shoulders and pulled him to her. He embraced her willingly, knowing soon they would be parted. He caught her off guard when he suddenly dropped his head and sought out her lips.

Gently he kissed her, and when she would have pulled away, he pulled her closer. Though she was surprised, she did not stop him. He kissed her sweetly, without expectations. It was a kiss goodbye.

The next thing Melanie knew, Samuel was being ripped from her arms and flung to the ground. She looked up in fright, only to see Merick towering over them. His chest was rising up and down while he took deep, angry breaths, and his fists were clenched so tightly they appeared white. He glared at them both, giving each an equal measure of his fury. Before he could speak, a swift movement caught Melanie's eye, and she looked over Merick's shoulder. Bevenly rushed toward him from the pathway and latched tightly onto his arm.

"My lord! *Reginald!* What is it you do?"

She knew well what it was he was doing. They'd both seen the kiss Samuel and Melanie shared. It was no accident they were here in the garden. Merick had sought Bevenly out and asked her to walk with him. When they'd entered the garden, she'd guessed he was going to seek out Melanie, for she frequented this spot. It had been a surprise to find her with Samuel. Bevenly saw the passionless kiss and guessed the pair had only been saying goodbye to one another. But Merick had lost all sense of reason. He'd rushed over and grabbed the poor man, brutally throwing him to the ground.

Merick was furious, but when Bevenly called him Reginald, he had remembered his precarious predicament. "How dare you touch your lord's lady!" he snarled.

Bevenly and Melanie both breathed a sigh of relief. But then, both were tense again when they saw that Merick was still prepared to do battle.

Samuel climbed slowly to his feet, unwilling to play the

part of a coward in front of Melanie. He stood before Merick and opened his mouth to spit out a retort. Before he could say a word, however, Melanie sprang forward and forced herself between the two men. Bevenly still had her hand on Merick's arm, and she tugged on him with no effect.

"How dare you, sir!" Melanie spat.

Merick was taken aback by her audacity. "How dare *I*?"

"Please, Reginald, you have made your point. Let us away!" Bevenly begged.

Merick shook free of her hold. "Nay! I will teach this prig some manners!" he vowed. Neatly stepping around Melanie, he balled up his fist and smashed it into Samuel's face, knocking him once more to the ground.

Both girls screamed. When Melanie would have run to aid Samuel, Merick stopped her by catching hold of her arm. "What do you think you're doing?" he growled in her ear. He pulled her over toward the rose bushes and stood in front of her, blocking Samuel from her sight.

Melanie caught a glimpse of Bevenly rushing to help Samuel. She knelt and took his head into her lap. Melanie turned her attention to Merick. She lifted her hand and slapped him soundly across the face. When he stared at her in shock, she lit into him.

"You, sir, are mistaken in what you saw."

"Do not deny he was kissing you," Merick warned her.

"I do not. He *was* kissing me — kissing me *goodbye!*"

Merick was startled. "Goodbye?"

"Yes! We are friends, and since Lord de Brock has decided to ransom me, he knew I would soon be leaving for good."

"No matter. He still had no right to touch you."

"Stop it, Merick!" Melanie whispered fiercely. She pushed

at him until he let her get past him. Quickly she rushed over to check on Samuel. "How does he fare?" she asked Bevenly.

"I am fine!" Samuel answered for himself. His eye was swollen, but he looked to be all right. "Let me up."

Bevenly tried to restrain Samuel, fearful he would challenge Merick. He was no match for him. "Lie still, please!"

Melanie knelt beside him. Merick saw her intent and walked over to stop her from touching the other man. When he snatched at her hand, Melanie slapped at him.

"Get away from us…you…you…bully!"

Merick stepped back when he heard the venom in Melanie's voice. No longer was he standing over a cowering man brought low by his fists. He now envisioned himself to be the helpless young man he'd once been, lying on the ground with only his sweet Melanie to protect him.

"By God!" he gasped. "What have I become?"

"That which you most despise!" Melanie snapped.

With Bevenly's help, she got Samuel to his feet. Merick did not try to stop her as she and Bevenly led Samuel down the garden path toward the castle.

~*~

"Please believe me when I tell you I am sorry." Merick had followed Melanie and Bevenly when they took the injured Samuel into Tenebrous to the physician's room. He had paced the hall while he waited for Melanie to emerge, only to have her stalk furiously past him when she did. He trailed after her until he finally overcame her hurried steps and pulled her gently into an alcove.

"The swelling in poor Samuel's face will take days to go down, thanks to you!" Melanie tried to move as far away from Merick as the confined area would allow. He was blocking the opening, and she didn't want to cause a scene by trying to get past him.

"I just lost control when I saw him kiss you!"

"And why do you suddenly care who kisses me? You seemed to have no regard for what I was doing over the past few days."

Merick looked abashed. "You know I have to put up the farce of training to be one of Dragon's men."

"That is a load of manure, and you know it! You love being here. You love it so much you wish you didn't have to leave. You're probably upset I'm being ransomed, and you fear I expect you to follow me. Well, let me tell you something—if this is any indication of how life with you is going to be, then stay here! Don't come home because I don't want to marry a bully."

Merick tried to touch her, but she only pulled farther away. "I am not a bully!"

Melanie regarded him foully. "It sure looked like you were, the way you were beating up on a helpless young man who was obviously no match for you!"

Merick couldn't help but puff out in pride over the way Melanie described him. Several weeks ago, she never would have said such a thing. "I thought you were tired of always having to rush to my rescue. Aren't you glad I can defend you now instead of the other way around?"

"Not at the expense of your kindness. Merciful heavens, Merick! I don't even know you anymore." Melanie's shoulders sagged in defeat. Perhaps he was right, she thought. She had wanted him to be more warrior-like, but she'd never suspected he would lose so much of himself in the process. She would give anything, she realized, to have him back the way he was before.

Merick put his hands on her shoulders and squeezed her

lightly. He took encouragement from the fact she didn't pull away. "I love you more than anything in the world. I just don't know what it is you want from me. You've driven me crazy with jealously while parading around with Samuel and complained I don't pay you enough attention. But when I do, you still are angry with me. Do you want a hero, or do you want a weakling?"

"I don't know!" Melanie yelled. She did push past him then and hurried out into the passageway. She fled toward the stairs but had to slow her pace and assume her limp when she heard others approaching. Wary of not having the blackened sap on her teeth, she kept her head low. She would have to return to the tower to get more of the sticky concoction. She'd dropped her other piece on the ground during the calamity with Merick and Samuel. Bevenly had been too busy fawning over Samuel to notice Melanie was suddenly sporting two front teeth. Bevenly had refused to leave Samuel's side and insisted she be the one to hold the ice pack on his swollen face.

Melanie climbed the sets of stairs to the tower as quickly as she was able. She could hear Merick behind her trying to follow casually like he wasn't coming after her. When she finally entered the tower, she went to push the door shut behind her, but Merick was already there. She allowed him in but ignored him while she searched for more of the sap to put on her teeth.

Merick closed the door and went over to sit down upon her bed. "What are you searching for?"

"Something to hit you with!" Melanie snapped.

Merick groaned. "How long are you going to be mad at me?"

"As long as it takes for the swelling to go down in Samuel's face," she replied smartly.

That could be a while, Merick thought, remembering the

long agonizing wait he'd had to endure for his own swelling to go down before he could come after Melanie. He laid back on her bed and made himself comfortable. "I guess I'll just have to wait then."

"You can't stay here. It's almost time for the midday meal. You'll be expected in the hall."

"They can do without me for a while," Merick said, unconcerned.

Melanie stomped her foot in frustration. "Get out!"

"I'm not leaving until you forgive me," he said stubbornly.

"Fine! I forgive you, now get out!"

"I'll leave when you kiss me," Merick told her, lying still and staring at the rafters overhead.

"You are positively infuriating!" Melanie walked over to stand before him, her hands clenched into fists resting on her hips. Before she could react, Merick suddenly reached up and pulled her down on top of him. He wrapped his arms around her tightly when she struggled to get away. "Let me go!"

"Kiss me, then I'll let you go," he promised.

Melanie had no choice but to comply. She gave a great sigh and lowered her lips to kiss him. When she was about to lift her head, Merick's hand reached up to tangle in her long flowing tresses and held her in place. He deepened the kiss, teasing her tongue with the tip of his own. Soon they were kissing passionately, and all thoughts of Merick leaving the room fled both their minds.

"I want you, Melanie," he said, his voice husky with longing. Melanie nodded her head in silent surrender, and Merick rolled her onto her back. As he lay over her, he loosened the ties of her dress and slid it slowly off her shoulders. He pushed it down farther, and Melanie had to wiggle to help him get it off the length of her body. He then reached down to grab her chemise and began pulling it up over her thighs. "I want to see all of you this time," he told her.

Melanie would not be denied the sight of Merick's body either. She tugged on his shirt to pull it from his breeches, and he helped pull it off over his head. She ran her hands lovingly down his arms and over his supple chest, admiring the thick muscles he sported. His body was browned by hours spent in the sun, and when he moved, he was stealthy, catlike, as though he was stalking her like his prey.

Merick straddled her hips and lifted himself slightly to pull her chemise up over her belly, then her breasts, and finally over her head. She lay naked before him. He sucked in his breath as he gazed at her beautiful form. Her breasts were full and high, with large rose-colored nipples and tiny buds that peeked at him teasingly. Her waist was slim, and he spanned it with both of his hands. She arched her back slightly, raising herself up to him temptingly.

"Love me, Merick," she begged.

He wasted no time unfastening his breeches and tossing them onto the floor. He then lay fully over her, resting his weight on his elbows. He reached down his hand to open her thighs and nestled himself securely between them.

When he perched himself before her, ready to make her his own once more, Melanie wrapped her hand around the length of him and gently squeezed his hardened manhood. She guided him toward her opening and then grabbed hold of his hips as he slid more fully inside of her. Slowly he stroked her, back and forth, and then his movements became more intense and bolder. He began to move faster, and she could feel herself beginning to lose control.

Melanie rocked with the frantic pace Merick set. She held onto him, digging her nails into his back as she began to feel a tingling sensation in her lower body. She arched her back, allowing him deeper access, and heard his growl of approval. Faster he moved, and then she felt him stiffen suddenly and hold himself taut. Melanie closed her eyes tightly and gasped as she saw an explosion of colors as waves of release washed over her.

Merick kissed her sweetly as he rolled to his side on the little bed, holding her tightly in his arms. "Just tell me what you want of me, and I'll do it."

"I just want things to be the way they were before. I want to go home. I do love you, Merick, and I want to marry you, but I could not stand it if you continue to treat me merely as your possession."

"I am not the man I was, Melanie, but I swear to you I will do anything to show you how much I care for you."

"I just want you to need me, Merick."

"Though I no longer need you to fight my battles, I do need you in so many other ways, my love. You are the other half of me. You complete me. I could not picture my life without you by my side. When we return home, and we no longer must pretend we are something we're not, then I will show you. I will spend the rest of my life showing you, Melanie, how much I love you," he vowed.

Chapter 19

In the days that passed, while Melanie anxiously awaited the return of Dragon's man regarding her ransom, a distinct change had come over Merick. He made a point of visually seeking her out whenever she watched him train. It wasn't obvious to others, but Melanie caught his secretive glances and loving smiles. While Tenebrous inhabitants walked a wide arc around her, Merick passed so closely he could brush her hand or thigh. When his comrades cheered him for braving her pungent odor, he would laugh and say he was fearless. Soon the men realized Melanie no longer posed a threat to their nostrils. In fact, now that they knew she would be leaving soon, they began to nod their heads in greeting, even giving out the odd, "Good day, my lady."

Melanie enjoyed not being treated as an outcast and began to feel accepted. She was now allowed to take her meals in the hall if she wished. She did eat the midday meal there but continued to take breakfast and supper in the tower. Kallie still spent time with her, but Samuel now seemed to favor another companion.

Melanie wasn't sure if his behavior was due to his fear of Merick or if it was from the new friendship he'd formed with Bevenly. The two were practically inseparable, and it cheered Melanie's heart to see Samuel so happy. It was also a good thing to see that Bevenly no longer trailed along after Merick.

The day finally arrived when Dragon's man returned with news of her ransom. Dragon called for Melanie to meet with him in the solar, and this time Melanie was less intimidated.

"I have received your ransom, half paid now for your continued safety, the other half to be paid at an agreed-upon exchange place," Dragon informed her.

Melanie was relieved. She'd had no doubt her parents would pay the sum, but the entire ordeal made her fretful. "When do I leave?"

Dragon looked at her with an unreadable expression. "I have decided it will be in one week. It took my man five days to go to Balan Castle to deliver the message, wait for the sum to be paid, and to return here. I will send him out tomorrow with the note as to when and where the exchange will take place, which will be halfway between here and Balan Castle. I will await his return with the confirmation."

"Balan Castle? You sent the ransom note to Balan Castle?"

"Aye, that is where I took you from," Dragon replied.

"But my parents don't live at Balan Castle. Who received the note and paid the ransom?"

Dragon walked over to his desk and took out the note he'd received. "It was signed by Desmond de Balan," he told her. Then he smiled wickedly. "Ah, I remember him, the *legendary* Desmond, the one I jousted with."

Melanie didn't like the smirk on Dragon's face or his tone of voice when he said *legendary*. "You mean the one you unfairly unhorsed."

Dragon gave her an innocent smile and spread his hands wide. "All's fair in love and war, my lady."

She could argue the fact the tournament was neither love nor war, but she didn't want to anger him, not when she was so close to leaving this place. "Perhaps it is well that Desmond received the note and paid the ransom," she demurred. "He will assure my parents I am fine."

"If he is the one to make the exchange, then I may bring you out there myself. Perhaps he'd like to have another run at me," Dragon said, with a glint in his eye.

Melanie was becoming angry again. "Was that all then, my lord?" she asked, trying to hurry this meeting along. When Dragon looked like he was about to continue his plans for baiting her soon to be brother-in-law, Melanie flashed him her toothless grin. The sap gave her a tendency to drool, so she really need not resort to such tactics. It worked like a charm, though, and before she knew it, he was ushering her out the door. "Only one more week," she vowed silently as she hobbled down the hallway.

Kallie was waiting at the bottom of the stairway when she came down. "What did he say?" she asked anxiously.

"I'll be leaving in a week."

They headed down to the back passageway behind the great hall so they could continue their conversation in private. "That is wonderful news, although I admit I will miss you greatly," Kallie told her.

Melanie hugged her friend. "You've been so wonderful to me, Kallie. I will miss you too. At least I won't have to worry about Samuel, though. He seems to be quite taken with Bevenly."

"And she with him. That must be a relief for you."

Melanie smiled. "As long as she stays away from Merick,

I'm happy. And she and Samuel do make a good couple. As do you and Dragon," she added slyly. She was still hoping to convince Kallie to tell him she was a lady.

Kallie rolled her eyes. "I can see by the look on your face what it is you're thinking."

"It wouldn't go too badly, I am certain. He seems like a nice enough fellow despite all his gruffness. I'm sure he would not harm you if you told him the truth."

"He wouldn't," Kallie assured her. "But I'm still afraid of losing his trust."

"I do wish you'd change your mind, but it is up to you. If you're satisfied to leave things the way they are, then do so—it's your life," Melanie told her, despite not being happy about it.

That night in the tower room, Melanie told Merick her good news.

"He says he might actually go through with the exchange himself if Desmond will be there. He thinks to challenge him again."

Merick laughed. "I think issuing a challenge will be the last thing he wants to do if Desmond is dangling a large bag of coin before him."

"Well, I'm glad you're not worried."

"I'm not. Dragon's been in an unusually good mood lately. I think it has something to do with Fontleroy, believe it or not."

"Really? Come to think of it, things have been quiet around here lately. I guess the man learned his lesson after his last attack," Melanie observed.

"Aye, well, we did take all his weapons and horses and sent his men back to him with their tails between their legs."

"Maybe he's learned to not incite Dragon's wrath?"

"Perhaps, although the men are becoming slightly bored.

The sport Fontleroy provided them with at least offered some excitement."

Melanie saw the look of longing on Merick's face and knew he fancied himself as one of Dragon's men. He, too, probably missed the chance to ride out and battle the enemy as he had done earlier, especially now that he was so adept with his new sword.

"Let's not talk about Dragon or Fontleroy anymore," Merick said, a heated look coming over his face. "We only have a week left before you leave, and I cannot join you for at least a fortnight after that, so we'd best make good use of the time we have left together."

He then took her into his arms and lowered her gently onto the bed. Melanie smiled and wrapped her arms around his neck in response.

~*~

In five days, just as Jamie had predicted, his man returned from his meeting with Desmond. He again called for Melanie to join him in the solar so he could update her with what was to happen.

"I have decided to take you to the point of exchange myself. If we leave tomorrow morning, we can easily be at the halfway point by dusk."

Melanie was relieved she would be spared from spending a night out alone with Dragon. Although she still worried about what might happen when Dragon and Desmond came face to face, despite Merick's assurance that all would be well.

"You do not wish to challenge him, do you, my lord?" she asked nervously.

Dragon smiled tightly. "Nay, I do not," he said. He turned and glanced out the window, appearing uncharacteristically concerned about something.

"Are you expecting someone, my lord?" Melanie asked, wondering about the sudden change in his demeanor.

"Nay, I just thought I felt something," he said, still staring out across the fields beyond the walls of Tenebrous.

The shutters were open, and a gentle breeze was floating in through the window. The day was clear and warm today, and Melanie could hear the inhabitants of the castle mulling about below. They were taking advantage of the heat, knowing days like this were numbered now they were getting into autumn.

Suddenly, a cloud of dust far off in the distance caught Melanie's eye. It was strange, but the ground felt as though it shook slightly. As she stared at the rising dust, she saw Dragon stiffen.

"Good lord!" he gasped.

The force of his voice and the way he gripped the windowsill sent a tremor of fear through Melanie. "Is it Fontleroy, my lord?"

"Nay, he could not provide a force such as that," Dragon said as the riders began to come into view. There were hundreds of them, from what he could see. Dragon grabbed her hand and rushed from the room. Melanie struggled to keep up with him as he began descending the stairway. When they arrived on the second floor, he hollered for his men. By the time they were in the great hall, the men were amassing.

Tristan stepped forward. "The lookouts have spotted the army," he said.

"Any idea of who it is?" Dragon asked.

"Nay, my lord. Not yet."

Melanie pulled her hand from Dragon's grip, but he led her to a chair by the giant hearth and told her to stay put before he went back to join his men. Kallie heard the commotion from the kitchen and hurried to the hall to see what was going on. She spotted Melanie and went over to her.

"What's happening?" Kallie asked fearfully, knowing something was wrong.

"There is an army approaching, hundreds of them, and it looks like they're heading right for Tenebrous," Melanie told her.

Kallie sunk down in the chair beside her. "Do you know what colors they wear?"

"Nay, they were too far away when I saw them." Melanie was concerned about the look on her friend's face. Before she could comment about it, she saw Merick enter the room and walk over to join Dragon's men. A terrible thought entered her mind. "Kallie, you don't think Dragon would send his men out to fight, do you?" All she could think about was how they had come so far, and they were so close to getting out of there. If Merick went out to fight, he could lose his life. Fate wouldn't be so cruel as to separate them now!

"If it is an army approaching, then no. My lord does not have villagers to protect, so he would not send his men out. It would be suicide against a force that size, despite the skill of his knights. Tenebrous is formidable enough to withstand a siege. We have stockpiled the harvest in preparation for winter, and we have many wells. We would be all right," Kallie assured her.

Melanie was slightly relieved, but she still felt concerned they could be facing a long siege. Desmond was preparing to meet her the day after tomorrow. If Dragon failed to arrive with her, then the terms of his agreement would not be carried out. Desmond might form an army of his own to come after her and Merick. She suddenly didn't feel very well, her belly cramped up, and her hands began to sweat.

Kallie looked at her with concern. "Are you unwell?"

Melanie nodded her head. "I am so afraid I will have to continue to be toothless and lame for many more months to come."

Merick suddenly appeared before them. "My lady," he said, bowing his head to Melanie. He also nodded his head in greeting to Kallie. "My lord requests you both please come with me."

Reluctantly, they both rose and followed him, worrying what was going to happen next. Melanie did not like the tightness of Merick's smile. He was trying to be reassuring, she was certain, but she could tell how concerned he was. She noted he was well-armed, with his sword at his side and a dagger hilt showing from the top of each of his boots.

He led them to a small storage room at the back of the castle. The door was locked. Merick opened the door with a key, and when they entered, Melanie could see several large barrels, probably containing ale. Shelves lined three of the walls, and on them were different sized wooden boxes. They looked old, and Melanie figured they perhaps held items which might have been brought along with the men Dragon had recruited.

"Why have you brought us here?" Melanie asked Merick.

Before he had the chance to answer, Dragon entered the room and closed the door securely behind him. The look on his face was grim, and Melanie felt a tremor of fear.

"There isn't much time," he said. He held in his hands a sack he must have grabbed on his way past the kitchen. He handed it to Merick, who looked at him questioningly. Dragon then went over to the wall, which had no shelves, and struggled slightly to roll two of the barrels apart. He then reached down to the floor and pulled up a wooden trap door that had been hidden. They all moved closer so they could look below to a narrow set of wooden stairs leading down into darkness.

"The stairs will take you to a long passageway that leads right into the forest. It is old, but I have recently been down there myself, and know it to be safe," Dragon told them.

"My lord, why are you showing us this?" Merick asked.

Dragon turned to him. "I need you to take them out of here," he said, nodding his head in the direction of the women. When Merick opened his mouth to argue, Dragon put up his hand to silence him. "I made a promise to meet Lord de Balan with Lady Melanie, and I am a man of my word." He pulled a folded parchment out from his vest and handed it to Merick. "This tells you where to take her," he explained.

Merick could see the resolve on Dragon's face. As much as he hated to leave Tenebrous now, he could not let Melanie face any more danger. He took the paper and put it in the sack.

"There should be enough provisions in there to see the three of you through the next few days. You will probably not make it to the halfway place on time traveling by foot, but securing you a horse right now would be too dangerous. You will have to continue to Balan Castle if Desmond has gone. When you reach Balan Castle, Desmond should take care of your needs. He was hospitable enough to my messenger. Tell him he can keep the other half of the ransom for any inconvenience caused."

"The three of us?" Kallie's voice was no more than a whisper.

Melanie turned to see the stunned look on her friend's face. She was pale and shook slightly. "Kallie, are you all right?"

"Nay!" Kallie said loudly, causing Dragon to look at her sharply. "You cannot send me away!"

"Reginald will keep you safe. I must protect Tenebrous from the army — I cannot assure your protection here."

Melanie was surprised to see him take Kallie tenderly into his arms and kiss her gently on the lips.

Kallie pulled back and grasped his vest tightly in her hands. "My lord, the colors of the army, have you seen them?"

Dragon looked confused. "Aye. But what does it matter who comes? It only matters that you are away—now!"

Merick took Kallie's hand and began to pull her toward the entrance of the passageway. "Come, we will return when all is safe," he assured her.

Kallie wrenched her hand away and quickly stepped over to stand before Dragon once again. "The colors?" she insisted.

Dragon looked at her with exasperation. "Red and gold," he finally said.

"My...father!" Kallie cried out.

Merick and Melanie stared at her in shock. "Kallie, no! Not now!" Melanie warned.

"What do you mean, *your father*?" Dragon asked dangerously.

Kallie fell down on her knees before him. "My lord," she began. "My love...I am not a maid."

Dragon's face was incredulous. "You are not a maid?"

Kallie looked up at him pleadingly. "Nay. I am Lady Kallasandra Botenay."

"A lady!" Merick gasped. He knew time was of the essence right now, but as much as he wanted to get away with Melanie, he was intrigued by Kallie's revelation.

"When my train was attacked, my maid was killed. I donned her clothing when another group of riders fought off my attackers. I knew not if the men who saved me were good or if they might be as bad as the others. I could not take the chance of revealing myself to them. Fortunately, they were kind fellows, and they did rescue me, driving off the first attackers. Then they brought me to you."

"I remember," Dragon said. "They left you at the gates and then fled. Tristan went out and got you."

"Aye, you thought me to be a maid when he brought me before you. I remember your words to Tristan. You said you could use the help around the castle, so you agreed to let me stay."

"All this time, you've lied to me?"

"I was frightened and alone. All I knew of you was your fearsome reputation. I felt I needed to pretend in the beginning, or else you might have cast me out. I am sorry, my lord. Knowing you now, I realize you would never have done such a thing." Kallie dropped her head in sorrow.

Dragon stared at her for a moment. "You could have told me. I would not have harmed you, nor would I have sent you away."

Kallie raised her head to peek at him hopefully. "Then you are not angry with me?"

Dragon pulled her up into his embrace. "I love you, you silly little fool! But now it looks like I am going to have to fight your father's entire army to keep you."

"Take me to the gate. If my father suspects I am here, he will first ask to see me. I will tell him we are in love and not to attack."

Dragon did not appear optimistic. "I suppose he will demand we wed."

Kallie smacked him playfully on his huge broad chest. "Who says I will have you?"

"I do!" Dragon growled and squeezed her tightly again.

When it looked like the two of them would never pull away from each other, Merick delicately cleared his throat.

Dragon looked at him, appearing surprised he and Melanie were still in the room.

"Ah, yes. Reginald. Change of plans. Lady Kallasandra will stay here with me, but I still want you to take Lady Melanie to Balan Castle."

Merick was still reeling from Kallie's announcement. If the approaching army was, indeed, her father, then Tenebrous should be all right. Dragon wanted to marry Kallie, so there should be no reason for her father to lay siege. All the same, he was anxious to leave in case things didn't go well. Above all else, he had Melanie's welfare to consider. Merick clasped arms with Dragon in a friendly farewell while Melanie and Kallie hugged each other. Merick swung the sack over his shoulder and stepped toward the stairway.

"God speed," Kallie said to them, as Merick took Melanie's hand and led her down the stairway into the dark passage below.

Chapter 20

Merick grabbed a torch from the side of the tunnel once he and Melanie were below. Dragon threw down a flint and watched as he lit the torch, bathing the passageway with an eerie glow. Dragon saw him look up at him and gave a nod. He waited until Merick had led Melanie far enough away that he could no longer see the light from his torch. He then lowered the trapdoor and turned to Kallie. He smiled devilishly.

"Do you think they were truly fooled?" he asked her.

Kallie went to him and hugged him tightly. "How could they not be, my lord? You are a champion at deception."

"Only when it comes to repaying a debt. Remind me the next time Desmond calls in a favor to tell him to go to hell," Dragon growled.

"He did save me from those vagabonds and brought me to you safely. You owe him much!" Kallie reminded him.

"Aye, and I shall be forever in his debt," Dragon assured her.

"The plan you two devised was so clever. It worked like

a charm. You have turned Merick into a warrior, as Desmond requested."

"It made it easier that he came to me as a hero instead of one in a group of players, though it was unfortunate he lost his friends."

"That was not your fault. You have no control over that fool Fontleroy, and you weren't entirely certain when Merick would arrive," Kallie soothed him, knowing how worried he'd been about the injuries his own men had sustained.

"I suppose," Dragon agreed reluctantly.

"And as an added boon, we also made Melanie realize she has loved Merick all along. Their love has proven to be as strong as ours — they will be all right."

"I could not have done it without you," Dragon said.

"And your men also. May God forgive us all for the falsehoods we were forced to tell! 'Twas a good thing my mother explained lovemaking to me so thoroughly, for I actually had to tell Melanie we had known each other." Kallie blushed a bright pink.

Dragon smiled wickedly. "And so we shall, soon," he promised.

"I was so worried when Melanie took a liking to young Samuel, Holden's man."

"Aye, your cousin did not fill his men in on what was happening. Too many people knowing the secret would have been dangerous."

"At least young Samuel has found love. He and Bevenly are quite smitten with each other," Kallie laughed.

"Well, he can take her with him when he leaves. One less troublesome female under my roof."

"Very funny, my lord. Now, shall we go and greet my

father? It was kind of him to allow me to stay with you as we repaid our debt to Desmond."

"I wonder if he regrets his decision. He did make it while still caught up in the euphoric throes of gratitude toward the fellow for saving you."

"Perhaps Father is slightly dismayed it took longer than we thought."

"Aye," agreed Dragon.

"But I did have my maid with me, and Holden."

"Yes, Lilith played her part to perfection, as did your cousin."

"Holden will miss Tristan, I think, and you. But he must be anxious to get back and start running his own holding," Kallie said.

"He learned a lot while he was here — I am sure he will put it to good use."

"Let us go and greet Father now, my love. He will soon be at the gates."

"All right," Dragon agreed. He pushed the barrels back over the trapdoor and led Kallie out of the storage room.

"I cannot wait to see him!"

"Aye, well, we had best hurry. We do not want to keep him waiting."

"Not after he has arrived to give me away at our wedding," Kallie agreed.

"He did not have to bring his entire army with him!" Dragon said sarcastically. He pushed open the heavy doors, and they stepped outside into the bright sunshine.

"Father always was one for a grand show," Kallie said as she saw the huge group forming outside the gates of Tenebrous.

~*~

Melanie looked up at the hill as she and Merick passed by. It was hard to believe it had only been four months since they had lain up there on their backs and stared up at the blue sky. She remembered how she had felt that day, the resignation she'd had about marrying her childhood sweetheart. The man who walked confidently by her side now was no longer the man he once was. Where he once walked in fear, his gaze darting about the land like a frightened rabbit, he now carried himself proudly, his head held high, his step easy and determined.

But deep down, he was still her Merick.

The loving, kind, and gentle man of her dreams lived on in the body of a warrior. She could not say she didn't fear the loss of young Merick, the man he had once been. But she was growing used to the man he now was. And though he was ever her protector and champion, sometimes she would catch a glimpse of his former self when he kissed her sweetly and held her hand in his.

It would not be much longer until they were wed and lived together as man and wife. Where she once dreaded their union, she now knew she could never have loved another. She would have continued fighting for Merick for the rest of her life if he had not changed. It was too bad it had taken such unfortunate events to make her come to this realization. She looked up at Merick and smiled. He never would have to prove himself to her.

Melanie looked up the roadway and saw the village ahead. "Might we go around the village, Merick?" she asked, worrying the alehouse troublemakers would be milling about, especially now, it being late afternoon.

Merick smiled wickedly, reminding Melanie of Dragon. "Fear not, my love," he reassured her. "I am not looking for trouble today."

The lump in her throat grew larger the closer they got to the village. Melanie could now hear sounds of uproarious laughter from a crowd. They would have to pass the alehouse to get to Balan Castle, now that they were in town unless they were to turn around and go back through the forest.

Merick walked on resolutely. The sword at his side and the daggers tucked in his boots did not give him his confidence — he knew he could handle any problems he faced without the use of weapons. Dragon had trained him well. Despite the long journey from Tenebrous Castle, he did not feel tired. He and Melanie had traveled at a leisurely pace, simply enjoying their freedom and each other's company. It had set his mind at ease knowing Tenebrous was safe. After they had exited the passageway, he and Melanie had climbed a great hill overlooking the castle — the very one Merick had first observed Tenebrous from. He had seen the army amassing at the gates, and though it was too far to see precisely what was happening, he breathed easy when he saw the gates open, and several men ride in.

He chuckled when he thought of Dragon being wed to Kallie. It was obvious how in love the man was, for, despite all his gruff, he was ever tender with her. The thought of Dragon wedding made him think of his own wedding. Plans must quickly be made. He had seen Melanie look at her breakfast the past few mornings with dread, and he worried about her condition. It would appear they would be welcoming a new arrival to their family soon enough.

Merick's thoughts were suddenly interrupted by a familiar voice. Despite the laughter and yelling coming from the direction of the alehouse, he could make out Desmond's voice. His brother had not yet spotted him and Melanie, as it appeared he was haggling with a crone over the cost of a bag of merchandise she held in her wrinkled hands. She waved it back and forth in front of his face, tempting him to purchase her wares. Merick saw Desmond finally give in and pay the crone. He took the tiny cloth sack and swiftly tucked it into his vest.

Finally, Desmond turned. At first, he appeared stunned, as though he could not believe his own eyes. He stood rooted to the spot. Merick watched as the crone hurried away, leaving him to stand on the side of the roadway alone.

Merick was relieved to see Desmond no longer needed the help of his crutch to walk, and he surmised his wounded leg had healed. He waved, and when Melanie caught sight of Desmond, she hollered with delight. Her yell broke the trance Desmond was in, and he swiftly began walking toward them.

"By God! Merick? Is it really you?" he exclaimed, as he came up before them.

Merick reached out to clasp his arm in a firm grip. "Aye, it is me, Brother."

Melanie could not be so restrained. She leapt at Desmond and hugged him fiercely. "I'm sorry we were not there to meet you to make the exchange, but we were forced to travel by foot." She released him and stepped back to stand beside Merick.

Desmond regarded them curiously for a moment as though he didn't understand Melanie's words. But then, as though he suddenly remembered the ransom, he nodded his head. "I was wondering what happened to you! I was just now about to return to Balan Castle and rouse up as many men as I could to go after you."

"I was so afraid you might do just that!" Melanie exclaimed. "I'm glad we caught you before you left."

"Aye, well, I thought de Brock to be an honest man— despite the questionable tactics he used in the tournament—so I didn't leap to any conclusions. I figured I would wait a couple of days and see if he sent another messenger to explain what went wrong."

"Something did go wrong. Terribly wrong," Merick said. "A lady at Tenebrous—someone de Brock had grown quite fond of—had been posing as a maid for some time. Just before Dragon was set to leave with Melanie to meet with you, an army descended upon the castle. It seems the lady's father had come to retrieve his daughter."

"Really!" said Desmond, appearing intrigued by the tale.

"Aye! The lady's name was Kallie—actually, Kallasandra— she was my friend. She helped me fall down the stairs, knock out my teeth, and drive everyone away with a foul odor."

"Some friend," Desmond said, looking at Melanie's mouth.

She flashed him a pretty smile. "My teeth are fine. It was all done as a ruse to prevent Dragon from wanting to marry me, which was a good thing because he really loves Kallie—I mean, Kallasandra."

"The lady whose father descended on Tenebrous with an army," Desmond reminded her.

"Dragon didn't know she was a lady, but now he does, and they are to marry!" Melanie said excitedly. Then a look of trepidation crossed her brow. "And what of your wedding to Beatrice?"

Desmond grinned crookedly. "I couldn't very well get married without my best man, now could I?" he said, referring to Merick.

"Perhaps we could have a double wedding then?" Merick suggested.

"Perhaps," Desmond said vaguely. He had broken off his betrothal with Beatrice shortly after Merick had left when she had stormed into his room and demanded he challenge Dragon to a rematch. But there would be time to talk about his love life later.

"Oh, how I wish we could attend Dragon and Kallie's wedding, and they could attend ours, too," Melanie said.

"I don't think that will be possible, my love."

"Aye, you're right. Then Dragon would know you're not really Reginald," Melanie reluctantly agreed.

Suddenly, a loud scream pierced the air. The old crone had been attempting to pass by the alehouse, and one of the men had staggered in front of her and knocked her to the ground. Instead of helping the old woman up, the man attempted to step over her but misgauged his direction and wound up falling across her leg.

Merick led Melanie to the side of the dirt roadway. "Stay here, love," he told her before passing her his sword and stalking off in the direction of the alehouse.

"Nay, Merick! Do not," Melanie begged, but she knew it was useless to get him to listen to her now. It eased her fear slightly when she saw Desmond walk up beside Merick to join him.

A group had formed around the drunken man and the crone, who was more angry than hurt. The woman attempted to struggle to her feet now that she'd forced his leg off hers. She shouted obscenities so loudly. Melanie had no problem hearing every word from where she stood.

The drunken fellow was helped to his feet by a couple of his friends, who appeared no better off than he was. The crowd outside the alehouse was laughing and began jeering at the crone, enjoying the scene she was causing. The old woman finally rose to her feet and attempted to leave. When the crowd blocked her way, Merick stepped forward.

"Unhand that woman!" he growled. Immediately, the man who had latched onto the crone turned to see who was speaking.

"Oh, ho! Look what we have here!" the man laughed cruelly. "The lord's young son has finally returned home. You'll have to clean out the chicken coop for him," he said, looking at Desmond.

Instead of getting angry, Merick smiled. He turned to look at Desmond, who had the same eager look upon his face. "Shall we, Brother?" he asked.

"Let's," Desmond agreed.

Before fists began flying, Merick quickly escorted the crone a safe distance away, then returned to join in on the action. The crowd became a mass of snarling, snapping, angry men intent on battle.

Melanie moved as close as she dared, trying to catch a glimpse of Merick. She saw him once or twice amidst a riot of bloodied noses and blackened eyes. It took less than five minutes before every man, with the exception of Merick and Desmond, lay still upon the ground. The pair stood back to back in the center of the fallen men and looked around themselves. They then broke into laughter and turned to slap each other on the back.

Merick brushed himself off and began walking toward Melanie but stopped when she suddenly cried out. He turned just in time to see a man rushing toward him with a long fiery stick he'd pulled out from a fire pit.

"Look out, Merick!" Desmond yelled.

Merick could see the flames flashing before his eyes as the man swung the stick maliciously before him. He waited, gauging his opponent the way Dragon had taught him to do—then made his move. He leaped into the air and spun right around with his leg raised high, kicking the flaming stick up into the air with his booted foot. They all watched as the stick flew high and fell back down, landing right on the thatched roof of the alehouse. It only took moments for the flames to catch and begin to burn the roof. The man who had held the torch looked at Merick with a mixture of fear and awe, turned on his heel, and ran down the roadway.

The owner of the alehouse hurried out a few moments later, alerted to the danger by Desmond's holler of warning.

"Is there anyone else in there?" Desmond asked, about to rush inside if need be. The flames were now licking their way down the side of the building, which was filling up with thick smoke.

"Nay!" the man replied, staring at the alehouse with dismay. "Get some water, fools!" he screamed at the men on the ground, who were now rousing and staggering to their feet.

"Stream's too far away," one of the men whined.

The owner grabbed what buckets he could find and shoved them into the hands of his frequent patrons. "Hurry up, ye bloody fools!" he yelled.

Merick walked over to Melanie, and Desmond soon joined the pair. The three of them watched with contained amusement as the owner continued to try and rally the men to fetch him some water. But it was already too late. The alehouse was almost completely engulfed in flames.

"Shall we go home, Brother, Melanie?" Desmond asked them.

"Aye," they both agreed.

They headed down the roadway, leaving the smoking alehouse behind. "Oh, by the way, de Brock said you can keep the rest of the ransom money," Merick said.

"All right," Desmond agreed.

"You know, Dragon was not such a bad fellow, Desmond.

I think if you were to get to know him, you might like him."

Desmond smiled. "Do you think so?" he asked. He did not expect a response, for Melanie had grasped hold of Merick's hand and was staring up at him with an expression of undisguised adoration. Merick was looking down at her with the same look on his face.

Desmond lagged back a bit and watched his brother with Melanie. A look of triumph and contentment washed over his face.

Julie is a long-time resident of Hamilton, Ontario, where she lives with her husband of 25 years. She has two grown sons who recently left the nest. Working in a library for several years inspired her to pursue her long-time love of writing. Please check out her website http://julieparker.yolasite.com/

www.ingramcontent.com/pod-product-compliance
Lightning Source LLC
Chambersburg PA
CBHW030307180626
46810CB00003B/957